My True Angel

Irshad Thalakala

INVINCIBLE PUBLISHERS

First published in India in 2018 by Invincible Publishers

ISBN: 978-93-87328-20-4

Invincible Publishers

G-120, Sushant Lok III, Sector 57, Gurgaon-122002

Opposite Kasturba Ashram, Radaur Distt. Yamuna Nagar
Haryana - 135133

Digitally Printed at Replika Press Pvt. Ltd.

For

My Angels in life.

Zulekha Ibrahim Haji (Mother)
Ashida Edakkavil (Wife)

Acknowledgement

Finally, my dream to publish the novel comes true. Thank you, divine mysterious spirit. This journey of writing a love story has made me thankful for love in all its forms that the Almighty has blessed me with. I would like to use this space to thank everyone involved in this process. First of all, I would like to thank Invincible Publishers and all its staff to make this a good product. A special thanks to Nitesh Chaturvedi and Irfana Shabeer for the wonderful feedback. I also want to thank all my friends and cousins for their valuable inputs and suggestions. I would also like to thank all the people who I've come across in life and who influenced me to write. Last, but not the least, I want to thank my brother Imthiyaz for his creative ideas. Please keep me posted with your suggestions and feedback on my email id.

You can get in touch at irshad.thalakala@gmail.com.

Chapter 1

I tried opening my eyes and had no idea where I was.

I was not accustomed to this place yet, and then the past incident struck me.

Yes, I was in a hospital.

How did I reach here? What tragedy had happened to me? Thankfully, I did not lose my memory and could remember every major incident that had happened in my life. I think it is better to go back in time to know who I am, where I come from, what my priorities are and what my approach towards life is.

My story is all about the three angels who crossed my path.

I was born on a full moon day in the auspicious month of Ramzan, but it is not necessary to start from there. Let me skip my childhood. My schooling and college years were spent without major events, but I was good at studies. The story starts after my graduation.

I belong to a beautiful state in India. The place attracts tourists for its natural beauty and has many rivers, canals, backwaters, hill stations and forests. The state is blessed with luscious greenery on one side and on the other side, it faces the Arabian Sea. It is enriched with beauty of religion as well. My place has an international recognition for cultural performances such as Kathakali and Mohiniyattam. Also, this is the state where when a guy fails his exams, he boards the first flight to gulf countries for job hunt.

Yes, you guessed it right. I live in 'God's own country',

Kerala. Four districts in the north are collectively called Malabar, where the Muslim population is large in number. I belong to one of the districts called Kasaragod and was born into an orthodox Muslim Family.

I grew up in an environment where watching movies is forbidden according to the Islamic faith, speaking with the opposite gender is forbidden and drinking alcohol is strictly forbidden as well. Restriction gives way to greater rebellion. Naturally, I was attracted towards the first two and stayed away from the third one.

My name is Iqbal. My parents call me Ikku. I completed engineering and was on a job hunt.

Like any other middle-class family, we worried what the neighbors and relatives say about us. My mother, Nafisa is a homemaker and father, Abdulla is a farmer. He got some portion of land from my grandfather, which he turned into an Areca-nut farm. He is a short-tempered man and whenever he gets bored with regular stuff, he scolds my mother as he thinks that it is his matrimonial right.

My father is a sensitive, caring and loveable person. However, I don't understand what exactly causes him to behave shrewd sometimes. Every person has some internal pressures and frustrations and they need to find a way to get rid of it. Some smoke or drink, some practice spirituality and some do yoga. Unfortunately my mother is the victim of my father's frustrations.

She is a staunchly religious woman who got married at the

young age of sixteen and was denied the chance of further studies. I don't know what her reservations were back then but the moment there is a discussion about a working married woman, I can clearly see the void in her eyes.

I am the eldest son and have two siblings, a brother and a sister. Both are pursuing their graduation. Being an elder brother has its own perks. My douchebag brother, Asif is a hardcore cricket fan. Like many other youngsters, he too was a captive of the dream of making it big in the cricket world. This completely ruined his education. No other person in my family is as optimistic as Asif. He talks as if he is going to get selected in the Indian Cricket Team the very next day. To tell you the truth, he is reasonably good. On his day, he can pull off the classic 'Rahul Dravid's straight drive'. But he always complains that genetics screwed him over and that he inherited only the bad qualities from our parents. My father was a handsome lad during his younger days, but was extremely short-tempered. My mother had a great deal of patience but was absent-minded. Asif turned out to be a perfect mix of both, short-tempered and absent-minded.

Fouziya, my younger sister is the 'Miss know-it-all' of our family. She has a solution for every problem. At first, it seems like an honest remedy for our problems but years of the same crap from her has scraped us from within. Sometimes, it turns out to be a big blunder too.

Trin...Trin…Trin! The landline rang and it was Sajid's voice. It was the intimation call for our evening activities. Sajid and Mustafa were my childhood friends.

"Buddy, get ready...I will pick you up in ten minutes," said Sajid.

My mom did not like any of them because they could not even complete their schooling, while I was an 'Engineering' graduate. Mom was worried that their company would spoil me, or in other words, she thought that they were not suitable for our friendship.

Every mother in this world thinks that an egregious friendship spoils her child. I stepped out of home. Sajid was waiting outside with his black pulsar. He loved his bike. The chrome on his beast was still so shiny, as if brand new. He was an ardent connoisseur of motor cycles. Every day he had the same routine, get up 6 in the morning, wash the bike till you can see your own reflection smiling back and then go back to sleep again. He breathed with a dream of getting a Harley Davidson one day.

"My mom thinks that I should have better friends," I said and Sajid chuckled.

The men who are less skilled or semi-skilled have a better chance of getting settled in a career soon because they do not have issues with taking up odd jobs, but the person who has had a decent education, struggles to find a good job, a job that can justify his efforts. A recent survey reveals that only 10% of all engineering graduates experience a smooth career.

On our way, we picked up Mustafa. I was amazed that Sajid agreed to seat an extra person on his bike. More often than not, he was the only one riding. We headed to a Masjid nearby where most of our friends used to meet. Sometimes we played games like carom or chess in our club.

Since it was a place populated with a Muslim majority, we hardly witnessed girls and boys wandering together in a public place. They exchanged their feelings like in a 1970s movie. Inland letters were replaced by SMS. I was still happy that for God sake, pigeons were left free to fly. Girls were scared to go to the restaurants or coffee shops with their boyfriends. Love, feelings, intensity - everything existed, but parents were the biggest villains to their daughters' love.

Any guy who could manage to get into a relationship was considered very lucky. Girls were hesitant to break the social stigma and were not ready for all the complications that a relationship could bring. Parents believed that girls might not get a good proposal later if she had already had an affair in the past. That was the reason why we were single and desperate.

Sajid was the one with the breaking news. "Do you know Khader, the guy who stays near Jamia Masjid, is in a relationship with a beautiful girl and they speak on the phone all night long. Lucky fellow," Sajid murmured.

I understood the pain in Sajid's voice as he continued, "I have tried WhatsApp, prank calls, Facebook friend requests, and chat messages. I don't know buddy, why I am so unlucky."

He was clearly pissed, but he was not the only one. I was also looking for someone to share my life with and like Sajid, even I had not been lucky so far. When we were chatting, a few girls walked past us. Sajid made his usual comments, "I'm really bored with seeing the same faces. I want to go to Delhi or Mumbai. I've heard that girls out there are not that orthodox."

“It seems my worst nightmare is going to be a reality very soon,” Sajid said. We were curious to know what it was.

He took a pause and continued. "My dad is trying hard to get a Saudi visa for me and it is likely that everything will be clear in a couple of weeks. I may not be able to escape this time."

"Every middle-class family has hopes and they depend on us. They have suffered a lot for us and it is our responsibility to look after them. I am planning to go to Bangalore and try hard for a job. If we delay any further, it might get difficult for us. I know that we are going to face tough days ahead but we should not give up and continue our hard work until we succeed." I shared my views.

I continued, “Screw that let us forget all this and enjoy the days that we have. We can do something memorable for us to cherish. We may not get an opportunity like this when we get busy in our lives."

Mustafa said, "Hey guys… don't be so serious, if we are determined then we will be able to lead a comfortable life, but these are the days that will always be special. Let us enjoy the moment."

To conclude, I continued. "Wherever we go, we should keep in touch and help each other in need."

"Let us catch up with the group and join the game!" Mustafa screamed.

We stopped playing when the evening prayer call was announced from the Masjid. After the Namaz, we spent some more time there and decided to try some street food before going home. Our love for food was the common thing among us. That fried, oily and unhygienic food was something we all had our hearts on.

"Shall we try Shawarma today?" Sajid asked in a way as if he had his pockets full that day.

Shawarma is an Arabic food which is usually prepared in the most unhygienic and unhealthy way.

"Come on..." We walked towards the outlet. It looked weird the way it hung, and flies enjoyed the raw part of the flesh because it was in the open.

Mustafa did not like the idea of Shawarma, and he said, "Not sure, how old this chicken looks. I heard a person died after having Shawarma."

It did not matter to Sajid and he said, "As it gets older, it tastes better. Besides we are all going to die one day."

This was not the only nonsense that Sajid had uttered that day.

We started discussing our plans about organizing an

event in our native place before taking our separate roads in life.

“Hey guys! Independence Day is next week. Let’s celebrate?” Mustafa came up with the idea and it sounded like a good one to me.

"Fantastic idea, we should make it big so that it becomes a memory for every Independence Day here after. Let us plan a cultural program and game activities.” I was enthusiastic.

Mustafa added some more thoughts. “Let us invite the priests from all the religions and try to spread a positive message in the society. What if, we include some fun activities as well?"

I started eating slowly because usually the one who finishes first pays the bill. I looked at others and they were eating slower than me. Damn!

Sajid was the first one to finish and he cleverly escaped. "Hey guys, I know why you both are eating so slowly. I have 20 rupees in my pocket. Kindly pay the remaining amount."

Mustafa said, “I have 50 Rupees."

Therefore, I had to pay the remaining amount. I had some cash in my pocket, the balance of an electricity bill payment.

I reached home and found Asif heading towards the dining table. He was very conscious about what went into his stomach. I joined them at the table because mom did not like me having fast food. Mom had made rice, potato curry and sardine fish fry. So, one can imagine how humdrum our lives were.

Asif was not happy with the curry. "Every day potato?" he asked frustratedly.

"Yes Mom, he is the future Sachin Tendulkar. You should feed him healthy food. Also, we should be taking care of his skin too as he must look good on TV," I teased him.

Asif looked annoyed. "You are jealous because I play well. I get gastric trouble every time I have potatoes. I cannot concentrate on my batting because of this."

"Yes Mom…this is true…I've heard that the wicket keeper behind him, faces a tough time."

I was waiting for Fauziya's suggestion and as expected, her valuable advice was ready. It was a treat to listen to her every time she opened her mouth. I mean, you never know what she is going to say next. Sometimes her big mouth actually spilled gold but the rest of the times, it was just downright ridiculous nonsense.

"Why can't you do yoga? It will help you improve both your mental and physical fitness."

I looked at her as if I had heard about yoga for the very first time, and she continued, "I suggested it to one of my friends and she has now improved in her studies too."

We reacted as if she had done something great, and we praised her, "Nobody understands Fouziya's importance and she does not receive enough recognition." She did not even realize that we were mocking her.

Papa joined the table and the light-hearted jokes in the room turned into serious talks. We never cracked jokes and pulled each other's leg when Papa was around. We were not frightened of him but that was our way of showing respect. It was not new as every time he would join in, we would automatically transform into more subdued versions of ourselves.

"So what is your plan?" It was a bullet directed towards to me. I knew that he was not happy because I had roamed around with friends all day and had returned home late at night. Like every Indian father, he thought that I was not serious about my future.

"Papa, I am leaving for Bangalore at the end of this

month."

I had been witnessing some change in his behavior for the past few years. He wanted me to discuss with him before taking any decision and ask for his permission before going ahead with them. I did not know the reason for this change. Probably he was feeling insecure as he was getting older. There was no further cross-questioning and I was relieved.

After dinner, we went to the courtyard. I sensed that Fouziya was trying to bring up some serious current affair topic. However, I interrupted her. The girl was impatient. Perhaps she had something to share, which she must have learned from reading the newspapers.

I changed the topic. "We are planning a big celebration on this Independence Day. We have so many games planned for the day and wanted to have fun for one last time before we settle for a new life."

When Asif heard games, he got curious. "What about cricket?" I knew this was coming.

I explained, "Unfortunately, we do not have cricket on the list." Then, I explained all the games that we had planned.

Fouziya was impressed and she gave some suggestions too. "I think it would be a good idea to publish a newsletter where people can write articles regarding Independence. What do you say?"

For a change, it was a good idea from her. I appreciated it. She was happy that I complimented her and she continued, "You are doing a good job."

Fouziya talks sensibly generally but sometimes she talks too mature for her age. Hence, she becomes the butt of jokes and we didn't mind making her one.

"So Ikku, you are going to Bangalore?" Asif asked.

"Yes, you can enjoy, I won't be here to trouble you."

They knew that I was going to miss them the most, as we had never been apart before. Life is a journey and we must keep moving ahead. The tricky part of this journey is that we take the ticket to some destination and land at another. It is awful when we have to leave our loved ones to pursue something important.

"How often will you come back to the house?" That was Fouziya's query.

I responded, "Not sure, perhaps once in a month." She seemed fine with it but I knew that she too was going to miss the banter.

Finally, the day arrived and all our guests reached on time. We scheduled the flag hoisting for 10 A.M. After the flag hoisting, we distributed sweets and invited the guests to the beautifully decorated stage. Our program started with the national anthem, followed by patriotic songs by little kids.

It was amazing to watch the *maulwi*, *pandits* and the priests on the same platform. We felt proud because we were the ones who had made it possible. The guests then delivered speeches. All of them spoke about the same thing, unity and harmony amongst all religions.

It was a beautiful message from all three of them. However, the reality is that it is easier said than done. I have seen the same priests favoring their community during elections, medical quota seats, pension money that the government provides for poor and the financial aid that the government gives to construct houses.

I have seen the same people fighting for quota. The very same people had issues in the previous elections because their community was not given enough seats.

It was nothing but sheer hypocrisy. However, we were glad that our event went well.

I murmured to Mustafa. "I wouldn't be surprised if they

make an issue of the fact that they were not invited first to the dais to speak."

We distributed snacks after the speech and invited everyone to the playground where we had different games planned for everyone.

We started the competition with relay, followed by a tug-of-war.

After tug-of-war, we moved to *kabaddi.* We had lots of fun matches and concluded the competition after the kids' game and distributed the prizes. It was a fantastic day and all of us enjoyed a lot. Everyone went back home happy and we proudly cleared the mess later.

I returned home and found Asif and Fouziya talking about something funny that had happened during the event.

Pointing at me, Asif said, "Look, our hero has come."

I could understand the meaning behind his tone as he had finally got the opportunity to mock me. I was curious to know what it was.

"We thought you were organizing the event, but we only saw you distributing snacks." Asif said and started to snigger.

I understood what he was trying to say. Even after all the efforts to make the program a success, I was not respected even a bit. I had it coming with all the cricket jokes and what not, I had it coming.

Asif was happy to rub the ugly truth in my face, "Ikku... don't worry. Even if nobody respects you, we both will respect you."

"Ikku was making sure that everything was done in a smooth manner. I saw him working hard in the background." Fouziya tried to support me.

It gave Asif all the more scope to pull me down.

Asif continued, "Yes, he works in the background

everywhere. He can show off only in front of us." I kept quiet.

Now I started thinking. "Did everyone ignore me?" It is human nature to expect some form of appreciation when we work very hard. Unfortunately, nobody had appreciated our efforts.

Everybody likes being special. Even in our daily lives, we expect special attention, appreciation, recognition wherever we go. We feel good if a beautiful receptionist greets us with a nice smile. Well, especially if she is beautiful, I said to myself.

Through the event, I understood the importance of recognition. Then I tried to do a self-assessment. There are people working hard for me, have I ever appreciated them?

After dinner, I told mom that her potato curry was awesome.

My mom looked at me as if I had gone crazy.

Finally, the day came for me to leave my hometown. We decided to have a small get together in the club. Usually, the club was empty. Only during holidays, people came to play cards and chess.

Sajid always had one thing in mind. He said, "This is the best place to get a girl."

"The girl should also feel the same. Have you looked at yourself in the mirror recently?" I teased him.

He said, "Brother, the girls in our town are conservative. I should have been born in the US." He continued saying something that totally required some censoring.

Then we cut the cake and bid each other goodbye. It was a strange feeling, I had the same feeling when I was leaving school and then when I left college later. We spent some more time together over lunch.

Mustafa said, "So our journey towards the treasure hunt

has started. Whatever happens, our friendship should be the same. We must keep in touch." We promised to meet once a year.

We all make friendships throughout our lives but the friends from our native place remain in our hearts forever.

My train was scheduled for 7:30 P.M. from Mangalore. Mom had prepared *chapattis* and chicken curry for the journey.

Fouziya ironed my clothes and packed them in the bag.

"From now onwards, I will have to do all this by myself." I was determined.

Asif went to the internet cafe to get a printout of my online ticket.

Papa started giving me advice, which included what to eat and what not to eat, how to cross the road and how to keep the valuables safe during public transportation. It sounded like he was sending me to nursery school again but I could also feel the care behind his voice. Love given by parents is unconditional, and they are ready to make any sacrifice for their child's future. However, why are the children unable to reciprocate the same to their parents? It is a puzzle that still needs to be solved by upcoming generations.

My taxi arrived on time. We reached the railway station half an hour early. Asif went to the shop to get a water bottle, unaware that mom had already kept a bottle of boiled water inside my bag. In the meantime, Papa reminded me to take care of all the documents that I was carrying.

The train arrived and immediately, Asif carried my entire luggage and put it on my seat. I hugged everyone and boarded the train. Then I looked back at Mom. I noticed that her eyes were full of tears.

'I am going to have a tough time, living without her,' I thought.

It reminded me of a Facebook posts I had read earlier.

'My mom taught me everything, except how to live without her.'

So, the journey towards Bangalore started like this.

Chapter 2

My train reached Bangalore at 8:00 A.M.. I was feeling drowsy, as I had not had a peaceful sleep. Then, I picked up my bags and took an auto. The one thing that I was looking forward to in Bangalore was its weather. Everyone had glorified how amazing the weather was in Bangalore.

The auto driver took off. I gave my head a rest and relaxed my legs. It was a frantic journey. There was very little traffic on the road as it was still pretty early in the morning.

"Sir, Bangalore does not have that old charm anymore. The municipality has cut most of the trees down for the metro track," the driver said.

Bangalore was named as the Garden City. Earlier people visited the place to escape the summer heat, but for the past few years, the average temperature has gone up because of industries and the pollutants they release.

We reached the destination and I climbed three floors up and knocked on a door. My college senior, Harish opened the door. He was in a hurry to go to the office. There was one more roommate in that old apartment of ours.

I was not very impressed with the place. Dimension wise, the residence looked not more than 500-600 square feet, with a single bedroom, a hall, and a kitchen.

I asked Harish sarcastically, "Do you remember the last time you cleaned the floor here?"

I saw some chicken bones lying on the floor, which could easily have been 4-5 months old.

I asked, "Have you celebrated anything in here recently? I see some cake pieces."

He said that they had bought cake for New Year celebrations last.

Oh my god. It had already been eight months since the New Years.

I walked into the bedroom and tried to lie down on the bed. After a few moments, my body started itching badly. Then, I smelled the bed sheet and understood the reason.

I said to myself, "It is risky to sleep in here."

Then, I stood up and walked into the hall. The room was really huge with plenty of storage space. It was delighful to me as I was searching for a place to keep my luggage. When I opened a cupboard, I found it full of beer bottles. Then, I went to the toilet. The closet looked yellowish and smelly. After looking at it, my urge to urinate vanished. I ran out of the toilet.

Harish understood that I was not comfortable. He said, "Hey buddy…that is what a bachelor's room looks like. Do not worry, you will adjust to this."

Yes, that's what I was looking for, to be fine-tuned with this shit hole. However, the fact of the matter was that I had a place to sleep and it was cheaper than most other places.

Harish was getting late for office and passed me the duplicate key. He said, "Bye, see you in the evening."

I took out the broom and cleaned the place as much as I could, then went to sleep again.

I had a nice sleep. When I woke up in the evening, I

stepped out to have some food and purchase some necessary items. When I returned, I found both of them sleeping. And that was it, my first day in Bangalore came to an end and by the likes of it, it didn't look very promising.

The next morning, I browsed the Internet available in the room. The toilets were dirty but the internet had good speed. I searched and found that a job fair was happening in the city. Quickly, I brushed my teeth and freshened up to finish other activities.

I noted down the address of the event. Bangalore is one city that is known for its well-organized public transportation. Unlike other cities, I had heard good things about Bangalore. I walked to the bus stop but the traffic was horrible as it was the peak hours. In the prime areas, it took almost an hour to cover 8-10 kilometers. I started getting frustrated as the bus was moving as slow as a turtle.

I said to one of the co-passengers, "I could have reached sooner than this if I'd walked on the road."

He looked at me and said, "Looks like you are new to Bangalore. You will get used to the city traffic."

I was the only one who was bothered, the others just sat relaxed. Most of the people had put on their headphones and were enjoying music. By the time I reached my destination, it was almost noon.

When I got down, many people were moving in the same direction. I was sure that there was a college nearby. As I walked, the crowd kept increasing that pushed me on to a huge ground where the gathering was unimaginable. It was completely packed.

I had watched a scene like that only on TV where thousands gathered to listen to a politician's speech.

"What is this crowd doing here?" I inquired from one of them.

He responded, "This is a job fair and everyone has gathered for interviews."

I lost all my confidence by merely looking at the crowd that had turned up. I returned home.

On reaching home, I realized that somebody had stolen my wallet. Papa had agreed to send 5000 Rupees to me every month until I got a job. I did not have the courage to explain to him, what had happened to me. Instead, I called my mom and narrated the entire story to her. She assured me that she would send the money without informing Papa.

I asked how she was going to manage all that, and she said, "You don't worry about it. I will take care."

The next evening, I met the third roommate. I shook his hand and introduced myself.

He said, "My name is Bharat."

There was a bag in his hand, and I asked, "What is this?"

He said, "We usually party during the weekends."

He opened the cover. There were two bottles of liquor inside, both of different brands.

"Do you drink?" Bharat asked.

I said, "No."

Harish said, "He is a religious person, and it is forbidden according to his religion."

We all entered the hall.

Harish said, "Let me prepare some chicken recipe."

He started cutting some vegetables even before changing. I understood the anxiousness in his heart. Bharat opened up a newspaper and placed the eatables and liquor on it.

It was 'Teacher's Choice'.

Harish poured the liquor and soda in. He gazed at me and said, "You can enjoy the coke."

I took a glass of coke and joined in.

“Cheers.”

After some time, their tones began to change as both of them were fully intoxicated by then.

It was fun to watch Harish. One moment, he was happy and the next moment, he was drenched in his emotions.

Suddenly, he could not control the depth of his emotions anymore and almost started crying. Bharat had a tough time convincing him to stop and said, "Why do you cry for a girl who is not worth at all?”

When he heard this, he was completely shaken up and cried some more like a baby.

It is human nature. I had observed that many times earlier. Whenever someone is high on emotions for a loved one, then convincing them that the other person was not worth their time results in that person losing all control and breaking into tears.

Suddenly the mood switched to joyousness and he began dancing. The floor started shaking. As it was an old building, there was a great deal of noise coming out of our residence. The owner, who lived on the floor below ours could not bear the disturbance and rushed upstairs. The door was unlocked and he entered without wasting a second.

After all the drama, Harish relaxed on the floor. He was dressed in a lungi tied in the South Indian style but he had not tied it properly. When the owner of the house barged in suddenly, he stood up out of respect. His lungi fell open and he stood in front of him, in his underwear.

The owner lost his cool and said, “This is the reason I do not prefer to rent my place out to bachelors. I give you a month to vacate this place.”

Yet again, my fate had some other plans. It had just been

a couple of days in Bangalore and I was kicked out of the house on the third one.

The next day, when both my roommates were getting ready to go out, I said, "I think it would be better if we find an alternate house quickly."

Harish said, “We are going to assign this responsibility to you. Do not worry, you can find it within a week.”

They were going to Cubbon Park and I joined them. It is a massive park where on one side there is the Vidhan Sabha and the High Court, and the other side is adjacent to the Chinnaswami International cricket ground.

Harish had maintained a stylish beard and I asked him,

“How did you crack the interview with this beard?”

Bharat’s response startled me. “What do you think? Does he work for a multinational company? Beard is not an issue in delivering parcels for Dominos.”

Harish did not like it and he replied furiously, “Yes, I agree that I work in a food outlet as a delivery boy. But he is not the collector of Bangalore himself. He also works as a sales representative for medical products.”

It was astonishing. "I am confused…you both are Engineering graduates. Have you done your graduation only to work at food outlets or sell medical products?" I asked.

Bharat said, "It is very hard to convince our families."

The next day, I woke up a little early and checked my mobile inbox. I had received an SMS from one of my batch mates. According to the message, there was a walk-in interview. The venue address was mentioned in the SMS. I tried to inquire more, but could not get any more details.

I quickly got ready. Suddenly, I remembered that I had not shaved my beard, so I groomed myself hurriedly.

I convinced my roommates as well and we stepped out of

the apartment.

Bharat was a sophisticated guy, who had time management skills, but Harish was just the opposite. He did not comb his hair properly and looked sloppy.

"I could not even freshen up." Harish complained.

Bharat did not agree with that and said. "I saw you in the toilet."

Harish said, "I agree to that, I went to the toilet, but could not finish my mission. It takes half an hour. Today I tried my best to complete it quickly, but I left the battle as I did not want to disturb your plans."

As I had done earlier, we followed the crowd that was moving towards the target location. Again, a huge crowd had gathered at the ground. The security guards were controlling the crowd. I inquired about the procedure to attend the interview. However, his response shocked me. He said that there was no interview scheduled there, and that someone had forwarded some hoax messages.

Bharat turned towards me and said, "This is the reason we lost all hope."

The days passed without any proper direction. One day we got a call saying that there was another interview, but when we reached the location, we realized that they were recruiting for call-centers. Sometimes, companies asked for an experience letter. At one occasion, Harish shouted with frustration, "Nobody is ready to give the job to a fresher. If you do not give a job then how do we get the experience?"

At most places, we dropped the resume and returned. We never got a call back from any of them. Finally, we realized that there was no use of personally visiting the location. We started focusing on interviews where only a limited number of candidates were asked to apply. That was our best chance, but with the number of unemployed people in our country, even this technique seemed to fail. Therefore, we began searching actively on the internet and browsed through the job portals online. The worst thing was that we could not appear for a single interview in those two months.

We did not move from the old place, as we could not manage the time. There was no point banking upon my lazy roommates. I decided to approach the local agents, as I wanted to get that issue out of my system. I woke up early one morning and opened my laptop. I browsed through the internet and noted down some broker's number.

Then, I reached the location as the agent had guided me on the phone call.

"I am looking for a small house for three adults. One bedroom, a hall and a small kitchen will work for us."

His next question was, "Is it for bachelors or family?" I said that we were all bachelors.

"We have limited options for bachelors." That was the quick reaction.

After checking out a dozen of them, I liked one. It was a two-story building with two individual houses where the owner occupied the ground floor and the top floor was rented out.

As I liked the house, we decided to talk to the owner. We knocked on the door and the owner himself opened it. He invited us in and offered us to sit.

It was a small house, but nicely furnished. He then started asking us questions. "How many people are going to share the house?"

"Where do you work?"

"What is your educational background?"

It felt like an interview, but I answered politely. I had heard that this was going to be quite bad, but the bad part was yet to come.

His final question was, "What is your name?"

I said, "My name is Iqbal Abdulla."

His expressions changed completely and he asked, "Are you Muslim?" It was a strange tone.

"Yes, I am Muslim."

He took a pause and said, "Sorry, I am not renting my house to Muslims."

It was bizarre and I asked for a reason. He did not provide us with an answer, and we left the house.

I felt very bad because I was denied something on the basis of my religion and faith. It was not good to generalize like this. I had wonderful friends from other faiths. We even share food from the same plate. I had excellent neighbors who belonged to other religions and considered us as a family. In addition, I had awesome teachers from other religions, who supported me.

The agent gave me a suggestion, "Sir, it is difficult to get a house in this area. Shall we move to a Muslim neighbourhood?" I agreed and traveled with him on his scooter.

We traveled for half an hour and reached another place. It was on the outskirts and seemed as if it wasn't part of the main city. The roads were pathetic. Small huts were put up in between the stalls. Teashops and kebab centers were there on every street. Bangalore, also known as the Silicon Valley of India, had a neighborhood like this.

I sarcastically asked the agent, "Has electricity ever reached this place?"

When we reached there, it was almost sunset. Masjid prayer calls were announced. After a few moments, it started in another Masjid and echoed with another one and it continued.

So, I understood that there were Masjids everywhere around.

Burka-clad women were carrying water back from the bore-well. After every alternate shop, there was a perfume shop. It looked quite enticing. Therefore, I entered a shop and asked the name of one of the brands.

The shopkeeper said, "This is a famous brand of perfume, called Jannathul Firdouse."

I badly needed a perfume to get rid of the smell. I purchased one and applied to my body. I understood why perfumes were so popular in this place.

I looked at the small kids where they were playing cricket in the street. As any vehicle would pass, they would stop for a while. I closed my eyes for a moment and prayed for those kids that they get good education because they hold the power within to change the face of the country.

The agent realized that I did not like the place.

"Sir, I agree that it is a crowded area, but the cost of living here is cheaper compared to other areas," he muttered. I asked him to stop the search for the day. Then, I went to the bus stand, but had to wait almost an hour before I got a bus.

I narrated the story to my friends.

Bharat said, "I think it is better if all of us go together."

Next day, we found another agent, who had better knowledge about the vacant houses for rent. Unlike last time, we decided that only Bharat was going to talk with the agent and the owner.

After looking for many houses, we liked a couple of them and asked about their rent.

He said, “Ten thousand, five hundred rupees.”

Individually, we needed to pay thirty-five hundred rupees

each, per month.

That was more than what we could afford.

"Please let me know the amount that you all can afford," the agent asked.

We all looked at each other's face and Bharat responded,"1000 rupees per head is the maximum that we can manage."

The agent's expressions changed and he said that it was very difficult to get a home in that budget.

Finally, he took us to the top of a six-story building where there was an accommodation made up entirely of asbestos sheets.

He said, "The security man and his family were staying here. However, they went back to their hometown. I can only get this place for 3000 rupees." We returned home.

We all had a discussion on our way back home. Bharat and Harish were initially reluctant to move to that place.

I started convincing them, "Even if we are loud there, the owner will never come to know as it is an isolated house."

Bharat argued, "I think that is a better place than ours. It would be a nice change. I guess we can deal with the asbestos sheets."

Bharat argued, "My salary from my employer has been pending from the pastlast 3 months. We need to make some sacrifice, untill we settle well."

Harish agreed, "Yes, it is true. I also may also lose the job at any moment of time."

Finally, we all agreed and decided to move to the new house.

I called the agent and informed him about our plans. I reminded him to prepare the rental agreement. We had to deposit Rs.10,000 as security.

The next day, I got up a little early and finished the morning prayer. Then I called a tempo traveler as that was the easiest way to transport our luggage.

I dumped my luggage in the tempo first, followed by the others. There was still a lot of space remaining in the carriage area, as we did not have much belongings to call our own.

We reached the apartment and unloaded the luggage. The security man stopped us and asked, "Where do you want to go?"

We explained to him that we were the new residents of the asbestos house on the top floor.

He said, "Sorry. You cannot use the lift."

That was kind of a deal breaker. Then we remembered that one of us had a job as a sales representative, another delivered pizza for a living and the third one was jobless. Therefore, we could not afford to decline access to this accommodation. We had to endure and had to breathe through the pain.

We climbed all the six floors, dragging the luggage. By that time, the agent also reached with the rental agreement. We handed over the security deposit of Rs. 10,000 and entered our new home. Temporarily maybe, I thought.

The restaurant food had become costly, so we decided to cook at home. We purchased a kerosene gas stove and began preparing a meal. Our first experiment was rice and dal. We were not sure about the ingredients and added more chilli than required. The outcome was very bad, but we all ate without saying a word. It was tasteless and too spicy.

As a result, Harish had to deal with an upset stomach in the night, but he was not sure whether it was because of the food or not. After some time, Bharat and I also had the same problem. Therefore, our experimental cooking gifted us with loose motion. It was a horrible experience, as all three of us had to share a single toilet. Just imagine the situation, how we waited outside the toilet for our turn.

What do people do when they are tired of job hunt? Some people plan for higher education, some prepare for competitive exams, a few try to get a foreign country visa to try their luck, some brave-hearts try their hand at setting up their own businesses, but most of them just sleep.

I was not doing any of the options listed. I used to wake up early in the morning and walk until I got tired. When I got tired, I slept under the tree for some time and then continued with the walk.

On many days, I walked till evening and then returned home.

When I felt irritated, when I felt bad, when I felt emotionally low, when I failed at something in life, I just walked. I had visited almost all the places in Bangalore by just walking. I saw garbage dumped exactly at the place where the warning board read. 'Please do not dump the garbage here. You will be fined.'

There was another signboard. 'Please keep the city clean. Do not defecate at open places'. A police constable was urinating right in front of that sign.

One day while walking, I saw an interesting sentence written on a board, it read, 'When the going gets tough, the tough get going.' At the same time, I saw another heart touching scene. One physically disabled person was crawling, trying to approach the bus stop. After few moments, a shuttle arrived to pick him up. He could not get inside easily. I tried to help him, but he politely refused. After a couple of attempts, he got into the shuttle. I saw the identity card in his hand. It had the logo of 'Tata Consultancy Service'.

I could not believe it for a moment. This gentleman was working with the number one software company in India.

I saluted him a thousand times in my heart. I could not get a better motivation for the day.

I decided to focus, dedicate myself and work hard to achieve the success that I was starving for. I went to a cyber café and checked my emails. There was a call letter from one of the prestigious CMM level 5 companies. I had three weeks to prepare and decided to try harder and give my best shot.

I reached the interview location half an hour before the scheduled time. It looked well organized, as there were limited number of candidates. They first verified my documents and then allowed me to get in.

The first round consisted of questions based on aptitude and I had one hour to answer. Some questions seemed complex but I tried to attempt everything as there was no negative marking. I submitted the answer paper five minutes before the allotted time got over.

I waited outside for the results' announcement. I was eager to know about my performance because it was the first time in four months that I had received an opportunity to attend an organized interview. In my heart, I was satisfied with my preparation, performance, and delivery.

After three hours, they displayed the results on the notice board. To my surprise, I found my name on the checklist.

I was shortlisted for the second round. It seemed as if my fate was finally taking a fortunate turn and that the city of Bangalore had finally decided to treat me kindly.

I crossed the first hurdle. The second round was the combination of technical and HR round. My turn had come, and I entered inside a cabin where a panel of interviewers was seated. I sat in the chair after taking their permission.

They started the interview with questions about my background and hobbies. That helped me to ease down and then they moved to some technical questions to judge my knowledge. Finally, after a couple of HR related questions, I was asked to wait outside for the results.

I was breathing fast and could not sit in one place. I started walking from one corner to another. After 15 long minutes, the HR called my name. I was extremely happy to hear my name. He shook my hand and said, "Congratulations. You are hired for the job."

That was the most beautiful moment of my life. I felt like I was floating in the air and was unable to control my feelings.

I had finally found my key to happiness. My pursuit had resulted into something tangible. I was on cloud nine and was oblivious to the world around me for some good 10 minutes. One of the HR members of the team walked up to me and requested me to fill a form. I did as I was told and signed the form. I was told that I would receive the offer letter copy through email.

While all of that happened, my mind was eager to inform my parents about the job. I intentionally avoided calling there because I was afraid to lose control over my emotions. I rushed outside and my heart felt light as a feather. I bumped into a couple of people on my way and did not even bother to apologize.

I started dialing my father's number, but out of anxiousness and excitement, I could not search the number from the contact list. I took a deep breath and tried again. Papa received the call from the other side. I was speechless. After multiple attempts, I conveyed the message that I had got a job.

I felt proud that I had made my parents happy. I walked in the lawn for around half an hour to bring myself back to reality. Then I bought a cup of tea and walked to the bus stand to board the bus. After buying sweets I got into the bus.

On my way back home, I thought of my plans. I wanted to purchase something useful for my mother from my first salary. Both my roommates were happy to hear the news and we went out to celebrate.

After a couple of days, I received the offer letter. My joining date was on the following Monday. I told about it to my childhood friends, Mustafa and Sajid. They both were happy for me. I was eager to experience new things. Also, I didn't know that I was going to meet my angel very soon.

Chapter 3

I reached the office campus at 8:30 A.M. The guard, after checking my joining letter, directed me to the room where the induction program was being conducted. It was a two-day program. On the first day, we were briefed about the company policies, timings, leave policies, medical facilities, and other benefits. On the second day, the HR verified all the documents and submitted a copy to the back office.

I was now officially a part of the company and was also issued an identity card. On returning home, I looked at myself in the mirror with the company ID card around my neck. That was a proud moment for me. After the induction program, there was three months of training to attend.

After every class, the tutor gave us computer programs to study. It felt as if I was re-living my college days, and I was enjoying it to the fullest. I also made a few good friends during the training.

On the last day of the month, I received an SMS that my first salary had been credited to my account. I opened the e-mail, downloaded the pay slip and verified the pay breakage component by component. After the income tax, variable pay, and provident fund deduction, I saw a decent sum of money credited to the account.

Even though the SMS and the salary slip had exactly the same figures, I went to the ATM and got a balance slip printed. Then I logged into the internet bank account and checked the figures again. I did this for hours as I was really anxious.

Harish noticed these antics and said, "Iqbal, the salary will remain the same, no matter how many times you check."

"It just gives a very nice feeling to see this figure in my account," I said.

Bharat overheard us talking and screamed, "Party!"

Harish said, "Hey, it is so boring in here, man. Do you mind purchasing us a T.V. set with your first salary?"

I said, "I might be able to save 18-20 thousand after all my expenses. But I wanted to purchase a washing machine for my mother out of my first earnings. I am not sure whether I will be able to manage a T.V. after buying the washing machine."

"Go ahead, Iqbal. Your mom will be happy," Bharat encouraged me.

"I am sorry guys, but I don't mind throwing a party tonight." We all went out.

I was so happy to be attending this office. Every day bought some new experiences. I finished my mini project and presented a short demo to the team members. Everyone appreciated my project and demo.

In addition, I did reasonably well in the exams and soon received the confirmation letter. However, I was little disappointed as some of the good friends that I had made during that short time span, were going to be let off. I was excited, at the same time, to know how real-time projects work. My tutor assigned me the UNIX technology. I knew that it was a powerful technology and was eager to make a career in it.

I had an excellent sleep that night. My phone's ringing disturbed the peaceful aura of the early morning bliss the next day.

"Am I speaking with Mr. Iqbal?"

"Yes, this is Iqbal here."

He said, "My name is Narayan and you will be a part of my team. I will send the location details to you over e-mail. Can you join the new team from today itself?"

"Of course, I can join from today."

I reached the office on time. The project manager Narayan came to receive me.

He greeted, "Welcome to the team."

He continued, "You will explore new areas here. Also, you are going to have so much fun."

He took me to the cafeteria and ordered tea for both of us. We had a brief chat regarding the background and he gave me an overview of the project. Then he took me to the project area and introduced me to all the other team members.

It was a group of 40 members and it was very difficult for me to remember everybody's name. However, I could not forget this one girl's name, the girl whose name I will never forget in my entire lifetime.

I shook her hand. She flashed a beautiful smile and said, "My name is Rubina Sheikh."

I felt as if an electric shock had passed through my body. Perhaps, that is what 'love at first sight' is.

She was beautifully dressed in a white kurta, red pajamas, with a red dupatta that enhanced her charm. She looked gorgeous in that attire. She was of average height and was extremely fair in complexion. I also noticed that a cute dimple formed on her cheek when she smiled.

While my heart was being hit by her mesmerizing

presence, she received a phone call and moved away to talk privately. Her hair bellowed out as she walked, like waves in the ocean. I noticed the expressions on her face changing as she talked on the phone. I liked how cutely she talked, her hands moving about animatedly. She was one of the most beautiful girls I had seen till that day. I felt disconnected from the earth and fell into a hypnotic state where I had the least awareness about what went on around me.

There is a feature in modern cameras where we can focus only on the object we wish to capture and blur the background. What was happening to me was something similar to that. I just wanted to keep looking at that girl and nothing else. The first thing that struck my mind was that she belonged to my community, and it is the biggest factor in India.

She did not cover her head with a scarf, but I could easily guess from her name that she was a Muslim too. This girl had cast a spell on me. I was unable to sleep properly. I rolled back and forth, tried to sleep in different postures. After trying for some time, I gave up and moved to the balcony. The sky was clear without any clouds, and moonlight spread across the surface of the earth. It was a full moon night and when I looked at it, it seemed as if it was looking back at me too. I tried to walk from one side to another, and the moon followed me. The entire city of Bangalore was quiet and sleeping peacefully, but this unknown girl had taken away my sleep. Remembering her expressions bought a sense of happiness in my heart. I had never felt anything like it before, it was very strange yet so serene.

Rubina was my first love. Was I lucky to own my first love?

Hundreds of questions attacked my mind.

"There is a good chance that she is already committed to another guy. She is such a beautiful girl and surely, someone like me must already have approached her. What could be her present status? How can I approach her? She looks like a north Indian girl who speaks Urdu. My parents speak Malayalam and have no idea about Urdu. Is it going to be a language conflict? Even if she accepts, will my parents agree to this proposal? What about her parents?" I thought.

My only strings holding my hope up were that both of us belonged to the same faith and were working for the same company. I had not even talked to her but was already planning our marriage. My mind told me, 'Ikku, calm down. Don't count your chickens before the eggs have hatched.' Obviously, the first step was to talk to her and develop a good friendship with her.

The next day, I managed to reach the office, but I was 30 minutes late. I had been a sophisticated guy until I met this girl.

I was so anxious to meet Rubina that I swiped the ID card in a rush and it did not work. I then waited for someone else to come and give me access. I wanted Rubina to come out and open the door. I could not believe my eyes when my wishes actually came true. There she was, Rubina.

She looked towards me and asked, "Why are you stuck outside?"

"My identity card is not working. I will have to call the security to re-activate it. Could you please swipe your card and open the door for me now?"

She smiled and said, "Tail-gating is not allowed." Then she opened the door.

I wanted to speak with her more but did not know how to start.

I just said thanks and we proceeded inside.

When I reached the desk, I started thinking, 'There are more than a 100 people in this development center. Why was it only Rubina who came to my rescue? There is definitely some spiritual connection.'

Love makes people act and think crazy. It is such an overwhelming emotion.

I then saw a middle-aged man working seriously on his desktop. He seemed to be solving some complex puzzles.

"May I know what you are doing?" I asked out of curiosity.

He did not understand my question. "Can you please explain what this software job is all about?" I explicated my question.

He laughed out loud and said, "I was 22 years old when I joined this company. I did not have any idea what I was doing then. Now I am 42 years old and I still don't have a clue of what I am doing."

That was utterly confusing, but he continued, "Don't worry. You will take some time to understand it."

I had a mild headache as I had not had proper sleep the night before, but that did not stop me from thinking about 'my girl'. Yes, she was 'My Girl'. My heart owned her within 24 hours of meeting her. I wanted to be friends with her.

"But how?" I thought.

"We both are from the same community. Why can't I try that angle?" I decided to play the religion card just like politicians play in India.

It was lunchtime and I entered the Food Court. It was a huge canteen with multiple counters; South Indian, North Indian, Chinese, American, Italian, etc. I chose a South Indian Thali and loitered around to find a place to sit. Rubina was seated at one of the tables. It felt like God took her wherever I went.

"Perhaps, God sent her to earth only for me," I said to myself.

I approached Rubina and said, "Excuse me. Do you mind

if I join you?"

She replied, "Of course not, please sit." I pulled a chair and joined her for lunch.

We were seated at the balcony and a light breeze complimented her presence. She had difficulty managing her hair. She flung her tresses behind her shoulders but after some time, they came back to bother her again. She lost her patience and untied her hair completely. Then, she took out a ribbon from her bag and tied them afresh.

I still had trouble striking a conversation with her but somehow managed to ask, "How long have you been working here?"

She responded, "I joined the company four months ago." It was relieving for me as I had finally overcome my fear of speaking.

It was a fantastic feeling to sit and have food in the company of a beautiful girl. I wished a romantic song to be playing in the background.

She opened her lunch box and the aroma of tasty home-cooked food spread in the air.

"Do you bring lunch from home every day?" I asked casually.

Her answer was not something that I had expected. "Yes, I carry lunch home every day. The food they serve here at these counters makes me want to puke."

I could smell some attitude from that statement. A large number of employees had their lunch from those food counters and they weren't as unhygienic as she had made them sound.

Most good-looking girls have this problem. They do not think about another's perspective while speaking. How could I continue eating in front of her, after knowing that she might vomit if she ate my food? I tried to convince myself that she must have said it out of her immaturity. I looked at my plate and tried to eat, but it was hard to swallow anymore.

According to my plan A, I wanted to divert the topic to the religious side where there was still a chance to score some marks.

"Do we have a room here to perform the prayers?"

She responded with a blank expression.

She paused for some time and asked, "Excuse me, what is your name?"

It was humiliating, not because she had forgotten my name, it is only natural that some of us take time to learn new names, but there is a decent way to ask if one forgets.

I called out my name, loud and clear.

"Oh, you are Muslim. I have no idea about Muslim prayer rooms here." I thought she would get impressed by my religiosity, but I had still not made any positive influence.

We finished our lunch. However, hundreds of questions popped up in my mind. Is she arrogant? Is she just trying to avoid me? Or am I reading too much?

The truth was that my first impression on her was a disaster. What is the way to impress a girl? Is there any particular quality that girls like? Is there any book that can help me? Is there any 'expert advice' that can help me?

My approach had not worked well. I needed to think and plan properly for the next time. Naturally, in this kind of a situation, our faith towards God strengthens and the frequency of Masjid visits increases. While returning from the Masjid, I took a one Rupee coin and flipped it in the air. I did not have the courage to check whether it was 'heads' or 'tails'. I knew that if the result had come out negative, my heart would not accept it.

The next day, my manager announced that the team was planning for a day out over the weekend and everybody's suggestions were welcome. After a team discussion, we decided to go to a waterfall nearby and spend the day there. It was thrilling for me as I thought there could be something special for me on this trip.

It was early morning on a bright Sunday. Rubina was already inside the bus. She occupied the seat beside the driver. Dressed in blue jeans and a white round collared T-Shirt, she looked very chic. That was the first time I saw her in a western attire. I could not decide if she looked better in traditional Indian or western wear. She was a view worth looking at, whatever she wore.

She had not noticed me till then. I was restless but hesitant to go and sit next to her because of the last experience I had had with her. Something in my heart drove me to get up. When I stood up, some other guy occupied the place next to Rubina and struck a conversation with her. Both of them seemed so comfortable with each other and the sound of their laughter irritating me to the core. Our bus stopped at the destination, from where it was a mere ten minutes' walk to the Shivanasamudra waterfall. Though I was moving along with my other friends, my heart moved along with Rubina.

We finally reached the spot. "It is spectacular," Narayan exclaimed.

That was the common reaction from most of us and undoubtedly it is one of the best waterfalls to visit in the rainy season. It was lush green all around.

In that serene and amazing location, something disturbed me a lot. The guy from the bus just wouldn't stop accompanying Rubina. He followed her wherever she went. The sad part was that Rubina also enjoyed his company. They even shared food. Rubina wanted to go down to the water and that stupid guy helped her. I looked intently at his legs and my only desire was to break one of them.

I was restless. Was he Rubina's boyfriend? Their body language told me that they were just friends. Even if they were just friends, she clearly liked him. She laughed loudly at his stupid jokes. Why couldn't I impress her the same way that the guy had done?

The truth was, Rubina did not treat me the same way that she treated this boy. She knew that I liked her. That is the complexity with girls. They usually do not care about the people who care for them. They often take those people for granted who try to impress them. They ignore the guys who are ready to do anything for them.

I consciously walked past her many times but she did not notice me. She came to relax on a solid rock after playing in the water.

I sat next to her and asked, "How are you?"

She said, "Good...having so much fun."

"Do you like playing in the water?"

She said, "Yes, I love beaches and waterfalls. I am from Delhi, and there are no beaches and waterfalls back in my city. It is a completely different experience here."

I understood from her expressions that she loved the place. I was happy that she started the communication on a good note. Then, she asked something about my family.

I asked about her family in return. "My father is a businessman, mom is a housewife, and I have a younger sister who is studying medicine," Rubina responded.

I was about to ask what kind of business her father was involved in, but refrained because it would have given her the wrong signal.

We should be extremely careful about these initial

communications. My next milestone was to get her mobile number. I was perplexed whether to ask for it then or to give it some more time. What if she were to question, why do you need my number? Then I would not have had any answer.

'Curiosity killed the cat'. I tried to suppress my anxiety, but my heart could not do it. It forced me to ask, "Do you mind sharing your mobile number with me."

Luckily, she did not find anything weird in it and we exchanged our numbers.

My daily expenses steadily increased as I was working in a multinational company. Earlier, I was using a single pair of formal shoes. After taking up the job, I purchased another pair of casual shoes. I started taking into consideration the hygiene factor when selecting a restaurant to go eat at.

Gradually, I started taking an auto rickshaw for my local commute. My mobile started looking old and I felt the need to replace it. In addition, I started getting irritated with recharging the mobile frequently. Finally, I got a new handset with a postpaid connection.

Six months earlier, all these things were luxury to me. All of sudden, they became a necessity. My expenses tripled. Now I understood why people who earned in six digits also found it difficult to save much by the end of the month.

My lifestyle had changed a lot, but my craze towards football remained just the same. How'd I spent my weekends? We play football every Sunday morning. I literally pushed everyone to the ground and it took much more time than the total hours spent in playing the sport. Some acted as if they were doing a favor by coming to play.

We could not manage to purchase the TV because of multiple reasons. I missed the telecast of all the cricket matches. There was an important India/Pakistan world cup match scheduled for the next day, but I could not find any place where we could watch the game.

Bharat said, "I know a shop on MG Road where there is a T.V. I saw a group of people watching the match outside the shop."

The match had almost reached it's climax when we reached there. The shop owner became furious when more people gathered. India required seven runs in the last over to win the match and exactly at that time, he switched off the TV. We badly needed a TV in our house but I did not have the money in my account. I eventually purchased it through my credit card.

It was peaceful for some days, and then there were communal riots in the city. One of the groups forced the entire city to shut down. We had purchased all the necessary items a day before. The entire street looked deserted as people avoided coming out. All the companies, schools and banks closed down.

All the IT companies immediately closed down because the management worried about the damage to physical assets. Most of my friends and colleagues belong to other communities. It was awkward for me to be open with my thoughts with them whenever any communal tension happened. My friends behaved the usual way with me but still, there was some discomfort. We played all the indoor games and tried to pass the time.

Some bottles fell from our apartment while we were busy playing carom. Perhaps, some kids might have dropped them. The police rushed to our apartment building and searched each house. Finally, they came to our place. We were still staying in the asbestos house on the top floor.

The Police Inspector suspected us, since we stayed at such a place. He asked us to get into the police jeep immediately and did not allow us to even change our clothes. However, I was lucky that I got a chance to wear my underwear within a fraction of a second, as I had seen in some movies how the police asks some people to undress completely inside the lock-up.

We entered the police station, and the Inspector questioned us for half an hour. He realized that we were staying in a mixed community and asked for us to let go.

There were so many houses in that building. Why had the police only targeted us? Just because we were a bunch of bachelors, who stayed on the top floor in a house made of asbestos sheets?

One question remained with me. There is a possibility where innocent people are targeted and tortured on grounds of suspicion only because they belong to a low-income group or that they lived in poor housing areas. They cannot come out quickly as they may not have a good educational background or may not be staying with a mixed community.

I was squeamish. I could not change the existing system, but I could change the house, so that the next time we would not be targeted. This time, we found a new house quicker, as we were ready to spend more money on rent. We finalized on a one BHK apartment and shifted to our new flat. We liked the apartment as it had all the necessary amenities.

I narrated my new love story to my roommates.

Harish said, "I think it will work out as you both belong to the same community."

Bharat's reaction was unusual, "Hello brother. It looks like an old age love story. You should find someone else if she is arrogant. Do you know how the modern age love story works? Guy and girl meet at the pub. After having a couple of drinks together, they decide to have a one-night-stand. If they like their experience, they move to a live-in relationship. The relationship continues as long as the intimacy is intact. If anyone finds a better option, they just break-up and move on."

Harish looked at me and started speaking seriously. "Do not pay attention to Bharat's words."

He continued after a moment, "If you love someone, tell her because hearts are often broken by words left unspoken."

Chapter 4

I was happy attending office everyday. Whenever I walked into the office, I took a glance at places where Rubina could be found usually.

Spot number 1: In the lawn area, where she often chatted with her friends.

Spot Number 2: Near the reception area, where Rubina usually read the newspaper while sipping coffee.

Spot Number 3: Outside in the balcony area, where she was mostly on the phone.

I did not see Rubina at any of these places and rushed towards the workplace. When I asked her friends, I came to know that she was on leave. I missed her presence. Though we did not share a strong bond, a smile from Rubina made my day. I always felt energized to start the day's work after that smile.

I wanted to talk to her but was not sure what she would think of me if I called her. I thought that she would get doubtful and uncomfortable with my approach and would start keeping a distance. However, I could not control the anxiety and dialed her number.

Rubina received from the other side.

"Hello Rubina, how are you?"

She responded, "I am not feeling well, so took a day off. Is there anything urgent?"

I thought it inappropriate to ask a girl the reason for her illness.

"Nothing urgent, I just called to ask about your health. I can tell from your voice that you are not well. Take good rest and get well soon."

"Sure, Iqbal. Thanks for calling."

The next day, she was at the office.

"How are you?" I asked.

"I am feeling better, but loads of e-mails have piled up."

I responded, "Yes, that happens…"

I did not want to disturb her. I said, "Carry on with your work."

My next step was to take her out for a date. But, how could I do it?

I did not have a choice but to wait for some more days for her to recover completely. After a couple of days, I met her at the lift lobby. I observed that one of her earrings hung loose.

I said, "Rubina, it looks like your earring is about to fall."

"Thanks a lot. I could have lost it," she responded, "This is my favorite one."

"Is it diamond?"

"Yes, it is."

I decided to use the opportunity. I thought that she would not refuse a date after I saved her favorite ear stud.

"Are you on your way to the canteen?" I asked casually.

"Yes, I am."

"I know a very good restaurant around here. Do you want to join me?"

It looked as if she was trying to find a way to avoid my offer. My situation was like an angler, who hardly gets good fish. I started to tighten the reins.

This time, I said in a convincing manner, “It is very near to the office, and I am sure we can come back quickly." She could not refuse and we made our way to the restaurant.

We occupied the seats near the lake. There were hardly any people in the restaurant as it was non-business hours.

"Have you been to this place before?” I began the conversation.

She responded. "No. I haven’t, but the ambience here is good."

It was a relief for me that she liked the place, but she still did not look comfortable.

The waiter came to our table with a menu. I ordered sev puri and strawberry juice, whereas Rubina ordered just a glass of orange juice.

I said, "North Indian recipes are delicious here. You should try it."

"No, I had a heavy lunch."

There was pin drop silence for some time. That usually happens during the first date. Rubina did not attempt to make friendly conversation. Maybe she was thinking that I was not a good match for her.

Nevertheless, I refused to give up and tried my best to strike a bond of friendship with her.

"What is your plan?" I asked.

She gazed towards me and I said, "I mean…future plans..."

She stammered, "Well…my plans…”

She took a long pause and then continued, “I wanted to prepare for CAT exams, but my parents are seriously looking for a guy for me."

That was an interesting topic to discuss.

"You don't want to get married now?" It was a prompt reaction.

She explained, "It is not that I do not want to get married now. It's just that my expectations about a guy and my parents' expectations for the same hardly match."

I was curious to know about her preferences. I wanted to make sure whether I was on the list or not.

"What are your expectations? I hope you don't mind sharing it with me," I said.

She said, "I am looking for someone who is handsome and smart, someone who is settled in the U.S., and someone who travels the world." My heartbeat stopped for a moment because I was nowhere on the list. I understood that she was ambitious and that is not a bad quality at all.

"What about your parents?"

She took a sip of juice and continued, "They just want me to get married."

She continued, "I am fed-up of looking at matrimonial profiles. I have already rejected more than a 100 profiles till now."

I agree that she was a beautiful girl with a decent job but she was not someone who could reject all those proposals that came her way. I think this is the problem with some girls who crack IT jobs. A couple of idiots like me propose to them, and then they start imagining themselves as the 'daughters of Prince Charles'.

When I was trying to understand more about her, she cross-questioned me, "What do you do on weekends?"

"Sleep," I laughed.

She replied quickly. "You don't party?" It was as if she

wanted to say, "Oh God! Don't you brush your teeth on weekends?"

Although I understood her question, yet I pretended not to and asked, "Partying?"

"Yes, Going to pubs and discos. I love to party."

"I have been to a pub with my friends. But I did not like that experience very much."

For a moment, I thought about my mother. Mom would faint if she came to know that her daughter-in-law goes to pubs. Perhaps Rubina was trying to convey that she was not interested in me. I just waited for the bill.

I realized that Rubina was not the kind of girl whom I had carried along with me in my heart since childhood. Also, from this little conversation, I could easily tell that she was a bit arrogant and had an attitude problem. I remembered an old saying that 'every rose has its thorn'.

So, my first date with Rubina was a big disaster.

I said to myself, "You bit off more than you could chew."

Saturdays and Sundays are holidays for IT companies. What do people do on weekends? Most of them party and drink throughout the weekend. Some go out for movies in multiplexes and malls. The common mantra is to work hard and party harder.

Americans are smart. They know how to get the work done without losing the money. Do you know how it is possible?

A skilled American IT professional charges $100 per hour for his work. They outsourced the work to India where the same job can be completed for $20 per hour. The Indian government thinks that they have imported funds from the US by selling the IT services but the reality is different. Americans have successfully exported their culture along with outsourcing of work.

You can observe an IT professional's lifestyle. He drinks Coke or Pepsi. He eats food from McDonald's, KFC, Dominos and Pizza Hut. He purchases clothes from Levis, Louis Philippe, and Lee, etc. He prefers using mobiles of Samsung or iPhones. The shoes are usually picked from Reebok or Adidas.

These are all American brands. Can we talk about successful Electronics brands without mentioning foreign brands?

The funds IT companies source by selling software services is all sent back to the US by spending money on all these brands.

We analyzed the lifestyle of one class of people. I would like to discuss the lifestyle of another class of people in India. These individuals are the ones suffering because of globalization.

Once I was in a barbershop and waiting for my turn. I saw a young man stepping into the shop.

He inquired, "What is the charge for a haircut?"

The barber responded, "It is 60 Rupees."

"Then, what is the charge for shaving the beard?"

The barber then pointed to the display that had the answer to his question written very clearly in bold letters and responded, "It is 30 Rupees."

The young man was still not satisfied, and he questioned further, "Suppose I get both the haircut and shaving done, can I avail a discount then?"

The barber had now started to get irritated, and he said,

"There is no discount in this shop."

The man persisted and tried to bargain further. "I don't have so much of hair. Could you please charge less?"

The barber lost his cool at his stupidity and said, "I cannot give any discount, you either pay the amount written here or leave my shop."

A similar incident happened after a couple of days. A middle-aged woman stepped into a restaurant with her school-going children. She had carried a lunch box with her.

She asked the shop owner, "What is the price of Idli?"

"It is six rupees each," the shop owner responded.

"The size of the idly is so small. I need three idlies. Can you please give it for four rupees each?" She tried to bargain.

The response that she got was, "There is no discount. You can buy them only if you are ready to pay the fixed price."

I was astounded after observing both the cases.

I had never seen people bargaining at salons or restaurants before. What made them think that it was okay to bargain at these places?

The truth is, they were just innocent and naive people who failed to keep up with the implied rules of the modern world.

They are the ones who are the sufferers of globalization.

On that weekend, I went along with my roommates to Wonder-La, a water-themed park. There was a wave pool, where artificial waves were generated using electric energy. I noticed many couples standing in that pool, holding each other's hand. I wished Rubina had been there with me. I always thought about Rubina, whether I was happy or sad. I could not imagine my life without her.

I was getting crazy. When I watched movies or T.V., all the female actors started to look like Rubina. If I went to the mall, most of the girls looked like Rubina. It didn't matter if I opened or closed my eyes. She had swept into my imaginary world. The worst part was that I could not sleep as well. I never imagined in my wildest dream that I would ever get so desperate for a girl.

Some good things also happened to me. Everyone in the office started identifying me. Everyone knows the beautiful girl and any guy who is seen spending time with her, gets easy popularity in the office. People noticed me chatting with Rubina in the lawn. They knew that we both had participated together in fun events; many times, they caught us having tea together; and they observed that we helped each other at the workplace.

One day, I was involved in a casual chat with my teammates when one of the members said, 'Your Girl Rubina'.

I was so elated to hear the gossip that was officially on the grapevine. Only Rubina and I knew that we were just friends, but I liked all the rumors spreading in the office. Everyone enjoys the status of being the boyfriend of the most beautiful girl.

During my college days, I had developed the library software that was useful to the college. I had received the 'Best Student of the Year' award. Still, nobody identified me there. I was one of the best football players during my intermediate, but nobody had recognized me then either.

Here I was, enjoying all the popularity at the workplace, all because I started roaming around with a girl.

I wanted to express my love. What could be the consequences? I started thinking.

There are three possibilities. First, that, Rubina might start thinking about me seriously, but the chances are very slim. The second possibility was that she might completely avoid me. In this case, I might lose her friendship as well. The third possibility remained that she might reject my proposal, but I could try to maintain the friendship.

I was unable to keep these feelings inside me anymore. I

decided to divulge them, irrespective of the outcome. If the response was positive, then I would not ask anything more. If the reaction was negative, then I did not feel sure of what would happen to me? I may lose faith in love and girls. I may get addicted to something or may become a workaholic and would not marry at all in this life.

I waited for a long time to catch Rubina alone. Either she was with her manager, or her colleagues. She took lunch with her friends. After some time, I noticed that she was working all alone and I went to her desk. As soon I reached, she got a call and headed to the balcony.

After a couple of minutes, she returned and said, "Hi Iqbal, what's up?"

"Can you join me for tea?"

She said, "I have something to finish. Can I call you on your extension after half an hour?"

Those were the most painful thirty minutes that I experienced in my entire lifetime. Each minute felt like a year. Finally, 30 minutes passed but she did not call me. I wanted to go to the toilet but controlled as she could call during that time. Exactly after 52 minutes, she called and we moved to the cafeteria.

I found a beautiful place to sit. She started talking continuously.

I interrupted her, "Rubina, I would like to speak about something serious."

Her face became expressionless. Perhaps, she guessed what I was going to say. I tried to clear my throat, but the words did not come out of my mouth.

"I want to take this friendship to a different level."

She gazed at me with a question mark on her face, "What do you mean?"

She needed an explanation, and I was bound to give one. I wanted to be specific, but at the same time wanted to express my love in the best possible way.

I said, "I love to talk to you, and I love being with you. Would you consider a serious relationship with me?"

Rubina pretended that she did not understand my question.

“What do you mean by serious relationship?"

I answered confidently, "I would like to marry you."

I was so anxious to know her reaction. She looked closely at me and laughed loudly. She received a call exactly then and said, “It is an urgent call for me. Shall we talk sometime later?” She walked away.

It was awfully embarrassing for me. Her laughing loudly and walking away made me feel horribly humiliated. I waited until I finished my work and then called her number but she did not receive my call.

I was restless and was in a situation where I just wanted to talk to her. She received my call on the fifth ring. I requested her to come to the cafeteria. We both occupied the same place and continued the conversation.

"I expressed something to you. Can you please be kind enough to give an answer?” I was so uneasy.

After a moment of silence, Rubina said, "Sorry, I don’t think of you the same way." My world became blank for a moment. I tried to control my emotions.

She avoided eye contact. "May I know the reason?” I asked.

She took a long pause and then responded after some time,

“There is no particular reason."

"Is there a possibility that you might start thinking about

it now?" I asked in a sarcastic way.

"No," she muttered, but in a firm voice.

Now, I was curious to know whether she had a boyfriend. I never saw her in the office with anyone in particular, but she was always on the phone. I had never probed about this before.

I asked her, "Do you like someone else?"

"No, I don't have anyone else," Rubina said annoyed.

The answer was not convincing. "I am completely fine if you are dating someone else but I deserve a reasonable answer," I said.

Rubina lost her temper.

"What do you want to know? Do I have a boyfriend? Am I dating someone else? Here is the answer. I don't have anyone else. I do not roam around with anyone else. I just cannot imagine you as my boyfriend."

That was a stinging slap in my face.

My dream flight crashed before even taking off. I was so disappointed after knowing her views about me. I would have been okay if she had given a genuine reason. It would not have hurt so much if she had given the reason that she was already engaged to some other guy. Sometimes, a lie is better than the hard-hitting truth.

There is a better way of expressing things even if we do not like someone. We can try to make the other person hurt a little less. It felt like someone had poked my heart with a needle. I began questioning myself. Was I so bad that I deserved being treated in that way? My love towards Rubina was genuine but unfortunately, she did not understand its value.

I needed peace. My heart was like an ocean full of waves and I did not know how to calm it down. I could not hate her, even if I tried my best. I think that is the universal theory of love. We rebuke and abuse whenever someone close to our heart treats us badly. We are still incapable of hating them.

How could I forget Rubina and move on with my life?

I tried to read books, but that did not help me. I tried to do yoga but failed to concentrate. I had never felt such kind of pain and depression in my life before. I got upset on different occasions during my college days. However, at that time it only stayed for a few days.

I could not find a way to come out of this web. Finally, I applied leave for a week and reserved a bus ticket to my native place. I traveled home after six months.

I needed my parents and siblings near me at such a time in my life. We understand the value of our loved ones only during the rough patches of our life.

The bus reached the Kerala border. I had never realized how green and beautiful my town was. Although my inner-self experienced the pleasure of going home, there was excruciating pain in my heart, which was hard to heal.

I tried to forget her, but the harder I tried, the more I thought of her.

I reached home. When I entered, Papa was reading the newspaper and Mom was busy preparing breakfast. I went to the kitchen and saw that she was preparing dosa and green chilly chutney. My parents were happy to see me as I had been away from home for so long. Papa asked about each and everything that had happened in Bangalore. We had so many topics to discuss, as my papa did not speak much on the phone. My siblings had already left for school. The life in Bangalore had taken a toll on my body and mind. I hit the sack after breakfast.

Fouziya and Asif had returned home by the time I woke up. The first thing that Asif questioned was, "What did you bring for us from Bangalore?"

"I could not buy anything as I planned this trip without notice."

Asif did not like the word, 'without notice' and tried to poke, "This guy has become an executive now. He uses words which are hard to understand."

Then he continued, "I just asked whether you got any sweets, the answer to which is a simple yes or no."

I ignored him and requested him to get some water. He responded, "Have you started drinking mineral water as well? We only drink normal water here."

Asif requested something so casually while I was drinking water, "Ikku, can you buy a bike for me?"

I almost puked. It is not a bad idea for a college-going guy to have his own bike. But he spoke as if he meant, "Can you get us some cookies when you return home?"

I replied sarcastically, "I will get it when there is an exhibition in the town."

"How come you thought of a bike all of a sudden?"

He said, "I have a tough time managing both studies and sports. I usually skip the last few hours of college to reach the game on time. My coach has said repeatedly that I should be more punctual."

I pretended to listen to him and said, "You are right. We should not try the patience of a cricket coach."

Mom advised him to come out of his fantasy world and asked him to focus on studies.

However, Asif was not in a mood to listen, "Ikku…the bike is important for me to manage both studies and sports or otherwise I might have to skip…"

There was a pause for a moment, and then he said 'studies'.

I said, "Looks like you are taking your life for granted." He continued giving his own explanations to justify his demand.

"Ikku, it is not like before. These days, a bike, an iPhone, etc. are the minimum requirement for a college going guy."

"Sorry, I was not aware of that," I said with a hint of sarcasm.

The list was not going to end as Fouziya started with her demands too. She knew the technique of making her necessity, the core need of the entire house.

She said, "Some of the things are necessary for home."

My heart started beating fast as she said, "Laptop is one of the items which is very much necessary for home. There is an application called Skype. We will be able to see Ikku every day if we install it."

Fouziya started beating around the bush. I began acting emotional and said, "I was not aware that you want to see me every day."

Then I taunted her, "Don't you have any other use of the computer?"

She thought that we were already impressed with the idea. She started tightening the reins.

"If there is a laptop here, we all can use it for Facebook and for watching movies."

I said, "Oh yes, you may get bored by seeing me all the time on Skype. In the meantime, Fouziya can browse Facebook and watch movies."

Now Fouziya got angry and said, "Ikku, you are working in a software firm. Don't you think it is a basic necessity in this world?"

I responded politely, "I agree that a laptop is the basic need of every home."

After a pause, I continued, "The way you have portrayed your need though, is not convincing enough."

"It is important to visit the *dargah* and we should be thankful for the divine power that helped us. I had made offerings at Ajmer and this is the reason you found a job so soon." The voice was of my papa.

I did not believe in all those superstitious things and answered him promptly. "You should have told me earlier, I would not have wasted any time preparing for the job."

He did not like my response and warned me in a tough pitch, "There will be bad luck if we make fun of the offerings."

Was everyone under the impression that I had loads of money? The general perception of IT guys is that they have a lot of money.

Mom was listening quietly while everyone else was listing their demands. "What about you? Don't you have any wishes?" I asked.

She said, "No dear, you just started earning, and you might not have a lot of money with you."

I was happy that my mother understood me.

I said, "I will not be able to plan the *dargah* visit this time, but we are going to purchase a new washing machine tomorrow."

The next day, we bought the washing machine and installed it in our home. Mom was very happy. In the meantime, Zubaida aunty visited us. She was my mom's sister-in-law. She was jealous, cunning and wily.

I always wondered how she found fault in everything.

Aunty observed the washing machine closely and said,

"What is the name of the brand? Oh, Godrej…"

She continued after some time, "My sister has Samsung, and that is a way better brand than this."

Fouziya responded quickly, "Aunty, but you do not have a washing machine. When will you buy a Samsung one?"

Aunty felt uneasy by the sudden verbal attack from the little girl but recovered from it immediately. Then, she pointed at the sofa set and said "All these materials are too old and worn out. You should replace them with new ones. Fouziya may not get good proposals if this is how she behaves."

Then, she looked at my mom and asked, "How old is she now?"

"My Fouziya is going to turn 19 this March," my mom replied.

Aunty reacted as if she had heard something outrageous. I was waiting to watch all the drama that was to follow and she started, "Oh, she is 19 already and you still have not started looking for proposals?"

Mom was speechless, perhaps she also thought that it was a little late. Aunty sat close to my mom and said, "Di, I swear...you will have a tough time, we should fulfil our responsibilities before a girl turns sixteen. It is hard to get good proposals once she crosses the marriageable age."

Then she drew close to mom's ear and whispered, "Do not tell it to anyone that she is 19 years old."

After doing the damage, Aunty came to sit near me.

She said, "Hello Iqbal, do you know my nephew, Salim?" I looked at her as if I had no clue what she was talking about.

"Hey, my brother's eldest son..."

I got a vague idea about whom she was talking, but waited to know more about the matter.

"Salim joined an IT Company and within two months, he flew to the U.S. When will you fly?"

I replied quickly, "He must be very talented and smart

and that is the reason the company might have sent him for rotation. I don't think I am going to fly anywhere soon."

Chapter 5

Although my friends Mustafa and Sajid were not in the town, I still enjoyed every moment there. I swam, played with friends and enjoyed my favorite food, but there was something that haunted me. I did not feel like going back to office. I did not feel like going back to the same place where I had to see Rubina every day. I could have forgotten her if I did not meet her again. Sometimes, I thought about switching, but it was not easy as I had already signed a two years' bond with that endeavor.

I started my journey back to Bangalore. I precisely felt like leaving heaven and moving into hell. I had to practice avoiding Rubina. I had to find the mental space in which Rubina was not an important part of my life.

My friends had different pieces of advice. Bharat had a nice one. He said, "Pain given by a girl can be healed only by another girl. Find someone who is more suitable to you."

But, I was not in a position to give another try to a relationship. I felt so attached to Rubina still.

I could not find a way to avoid Rubina. I reached the office, and the first person that I met in the office was none other than her. She passed me by but pretended to not have seen me. I went to my desk and started checking my emails.

Again, my stupid mind thought about her, my heart expected a standard gesture from her. I was unable to do any work and dialed her extension number.

"Hello Rubina, do you mind coming for coffee?"

"Sorry Iqbal. I am very busy at this moment."

That was a bizarre reaction. Naturally, that sounded like she was avoiding me.

I asked myself so many questions, "What am I doing? She said in simple words that she is not interested. Why am I disturbing her again? Why can't I just move on with my life? I have already decided to assume that Rubina does not exist and that I never met her. But why can't I ensure that? Why do I feel like calling her repeatedly? Why does my heart not follow the instructions of my mind?"

Rubina was playing games on her mobile during the lunch break.

I politely started the conversation. "I would like to talk to you."

"Yes, talk to me." Her response was as fast as a bullet.

"Not here, can you please come to the canteen?"

"You can speak in front of everyone. I do not have anything private to talk." It was rude.

The male chauvinist in me felt insulted. I tried to control and said, "If we are speaking privately, it does not mean that we are talking about something in secret. Please come to the canteen."

Rubina agreed to come to the cafeteria when everyone else started noticing us.

She said, "Yes, go on…what you want to talk about?"

I took a deep breath and started, "I was not disappointed because of your answer. I genuinely tried to avoid you, but could not do it. The most difficult thing is, I cannot endure the hurt and can't even control myself when you ignore me."

"What do you want me to do?" The response was as blunt as before.

"I don't know. There is one more thing that haunts me. You did not give a proper reason..."

She replied with her usual arrogance, "It does not matter what reason I have." She walked out.

Why did I call her? I wanted to convey to Rubina that I was all right without her but I needed closure to come out of that mess. I requested her to be my friend until I was okay with the reality that she did not reciprocate my love. She got irritated with my presence. Forget about considering me for a boyfriend, she was not even ready to treat me as a human. Forget about sharing a life, she was not even willing to share a cup of tea.

That was the toughest phase of my life. Is this the deepest pain a person can experience? I don't think so. I think the greatest agony is when a parent loses their child. On the other hand, I think maybe losing an organ for a person is an immense suffering. I knew that my problem could be healed over a period of time. But, I was unable to concentrate on my work. Neither did I feel like eating, playing with friends nor doing any other bustles.

For a couple of months, I concentrated only on my work and never bothered to inquire about Rubina. Then, the Navratri festival approached. The company decided to celebrate with all the fun activities. A cultural dance program was planned, and all the employees participated in different activities. I saw Rubina enjoying with her friends.

She danced across the floor with her friends and mingled with everyone so casually. She was the center of attraction in the whole celebration. Again, my heart felt the same old feelings.

“How could she be so happy after putting me into this state?” My heart whispered.

I blocked her way and tried to talk to her.

It was a bizarre reaction from Rubina. "Excuse me, what do you want?"

I said politely, “I have some questions that are still not answered.”

“Iqbal...you have so many questions. May I ask a single question? Why should I give any explanations to you? Who are you to me?"

“Why do you treat me like your enemy?” I responded sulking.

“Look Iqbal, I do not treat you as my enemy. Honestly,

I am not comfortable answering some questions."

“Excuse me.” I did not have any idea about what she said.

She did not respond, instead said something else.

“I did not like the way you blocked my path.”

"The reason is...I had...I had something to say.”

I stammered.

“I don’t know. I feel so uncomfortable and I feel like you are stalking me." She then walked away.

That was absurd. I respected every girl and her emotions. I never stalked Rubina. I had a genuine feeling while proposing to her. It is also true that I tried my best to move on in my life when she rejected my love. Sometimes, I tried to talk to her because we both were working in the same company. I am a human being and not a saint. I could not behave as if a person was nonexistent if that person was very much alive and walking in front of me. I would have quit the company if I had a secure financial background.

I blocked her path again.

I questioned her, “How can you say that I stalked you? Tell me one instance when I misbehaved with you. You always treat me so badly."

She responded, “The word stalking could have different meanings for you and me. According to me, a guy blocking the girl's path is called stalking.”

“I had something to clarify whenever I approached you."

I wanted to change the perception that she carried in her mind about me. She thought that I am a person who did not value women. The bottom line was that I could not create an environment where there could be a healthy conversation between us. I failed miserably, but I gave it another shot.

"Rubina, I need your help to come out of this mess."

I waited for her response. She said, “It seems childish to me. A person asking for help to come out of depression. I am not a doctor or a psychiatrist to be able to help you."

She took a pause and continued, "Listen Iqbal, I am sure that you will find yourself a very good girl. I am not prepared for the mess in your head, so please just leave me alone. Let us please set our boundaries as strangers.”

She started making the move, and then came back a couple of steps and spoke out a strong warning, "If this is repeated, I will not have a other choice but to report to the management. I am sure you love this job and do not want to throw it away."

Had I tried to explain my feelings to someone who did not have a heart? How could anyone become so egocentric? This was the second time when she had threatened me that she would report to the higher management. I was not even worried about my mortality at that point of time. Neither a doctor, nor a psychiatrist, only Rubina could have helped me coming out of this chaos.

My primary purpose of going back to her was to make

her understand about my character, but I came to know her character very well. I asked myself that in India with the number two in world population, out of which, 50% must be women, then why didn't I get a girl who did not have such attitude? How many girls must I have seen in these 22 years? Why did this girl alone fascinate me?

The first thing that attracted me must have been her beauty. Then my subconscious mind must have told me that I was fit to get married. I had a degree and a decent job. She belonged to my community, which could easily be the striking reason to strengthen the feelings. I knew my parents, and how it was impossible for them to accept someone who did not belong to our community. All these were the factors that make my feelings stronger for her.

I continued asking questions to myself. "Is it possible to love another girl? What if I get married to another girl, can I do justice to her? Am I going to suffer like this throughout my life? Does true love happen only once in a lifetime? Will I have the same intensity, if I find another love? Will I ever sleep as peacefully as I used to before I met Rubina?"

I did not know the answer to any of those questions, nor did I know anyone who had the answers.

Also, I could not digest the fact that Rubina provoked my self-respect. I was unable to forget and forgive it easily. The last time, I had approached her with the intention of explaining my perspective about women to her. She dragged me further down each time I went up to her. I was crazy to want to talk to her once again.

There was no point in stocking this frustration inside me. She had no right to put me down. She was nobody to ridicule my emotions. I wanted to talk to her in such a way that I would not regret it. I was not worried about the consequences.

I went to Rubina's desk during the break. She was having

lunch and looked at me with a weird expression.

"I am not here for an argument. I just want to talk to you... probably this is the last time, I...I will not pester you after this, and this is my promise..."

"I have a busy schedule. Also, there is nothing to talk." Rubina's response was cold as usual.

“Rubina, you never allow me to speak. At least, I deserve that much.”

She said, “Okay, shall we meet at 5 P.M.? But, I cannot come to the canteen."

"That is fine. Can you come to the lawn area?” She nodded in acceptance.

She came to the lawn area where I was waiting for her.

I gestured and said, "Take a seat."

We both settled down and started the conversation.

I decided to keep the tone and expression normal.

I said, “What do you think of yourself?"

Rubina was shocked after listening to my question

and responded with a confused and insulted expression,

"What do you mean?”

I was on the ball. I continued, "Do you think that you are Aishwarya Rai?” I did not wait for the answer and continued, "You behave the same way.”

She responded, “What do you mean? Do I act like a star? When did I show you attitude?"

She did not allow me to speak and continued, "Please find someone else. I will help you find someone else."

I said, "Do you really think that I am desperately looking for some girl."

She dominated the conversation and did not allow me to

say another word. She said, "I feel like I am inside a cooking vessel if someone controls me. I cannot even go for a cup of tea with someone I don't like. I warned you many times to leave me alone. I do not understand why you behave like this. Sometimes you act like a mad dog."

The last sentence shattered me to pieces.

I was so furious and was breathing fast. I raised my hand with the intention of slapping her but my self-respect and ethics did not allow it.

She still found it offensive. After a few moments, she muttered, "You will regret this." She then rushed back towards her desk.

The next day, I reached office and smelled something fishy. I sensed a difference in people's behavior towards me and realized that almost everyone in the team had become aware of the incident.

One of the faithful team members came and shouted at me, "What crap have you done? It seems like Rubina is going to complain against you. Do you have any idea about the consequences?"

He continued, "Just call her and beg her not to complain." I was in no mood to listen and was totally prepared for the consequences.

After some time, I received a phone call from my manager and he asked me to meet him in one of the conference rooms. He wanted to speak with me privately.

He started, "I received a phone call from the HR management saying that Rubina has filed a complaint against you for harassment. This is a serious offence and against the company policy."

My manager paused for some time and then continued, "I understand that you had genuine feelings towards her but there is a strict policy when it comes to female employees."

I felt like he was trying to help me. He said, "You should make all attempts to push her to withdraw the complaint that she has already submitted. Otherwise, there is a clear threat to your job."

As expected, I received a call from the HR Manager and scheduled a meeting immediately in one of the rooms. I entered the hall and noticed that three senior management level executives were already present.

One of the executives started the conversation. "We have received a written complaint from one of our female employees, Rubina. She has mentioned in the complaint that you continuously harass her. On one occasion, you even raised your hand. She mentioned the name of four employees who witnessed this act. We are going to take confirmation from those employees. Before that, we would like to hear an explanation from your side."

I cleared my throat and started the conversation, "It is true that I raised my hand. But the provocation was from..."

Another executive interrupted me before completing the sentence and said, "We are not here to find out the reason behind the act. You have already admitted to doing it. If she provoked you, you should have informed the reporting manager or the HR Manager. The company has zero tolerance for harassment towards women employees. Please read the organizational rules and policies."

I took a deep breath and said, "She never listened to what I was trying to explain."

One of the executives responded, "We are not seeking justification. Rubina lodged a complaint saying that you used abusive words against her. Do you concur? It is a serious offence according to the organizational policy."

I understood that there was no point giving my statement there. It seemed like they had already decided what they wanted to do and just needed my statement for formality. I did not wait to conclude the conversation and walked out of the room.

My reporting manager still talked positively. "Rubina should withdraw her complaint, that is the only way to save your job."

I said, "Thank you for your kindness. My self-respect does not allow me to go to Rubina and beg her to withdraw the complaint. I am ready to face the actions taken against me by the management."

After some time, a couple of HR executives came to my desk. They held some papers with them and one of them said, "According to the organizational policy, we have to expel you without notice. Here is the separation letter." They handed over the separation letter to me.

He continued, "As per the agreement between you and the company, if anyone is terminating the employment, the other party must give three months of notice or equivalent amount of salary. We are giving three months of salary instead of three months of service." I was then handed over the cheque that had three months of salary.

I could not believe what was happening around me. I had expected some drama when I reached the office that morning. However, I never expected it to be my last day in the company.

The HR continued, "You will receive the outstanding salary along with the final settlement. You should return a couple of books that you owe the library. Also, you should return the desk key. You have 30 minutes to clear out."

I had heard that IT companies sacked their employees without notice but I had never expected even in my wildest dreams that something like this could happen to me. All this happened in just four hours and I understood how easy it was for the IT company to terminate its employees. I logged into my machine, connected to the network. Then, I opened the Outlook Express and composed an e-mail to Rubina.

My Dearest Rubina,

This is my final communication with you. I wanted to speak in person but it is not possible now. I cannot swallow my anger anymore. I should flush it out to get rid of my emotions.

I did not get hurt because you said 'No' to me. That is your personal choice. I respect it, and you have the full right to choose the one you like.

I was completely broken due to the way you treated me. It was humiliating. It is the height of hurt one can experience, coming from someone whom he adores so much.

Perhaps I was a fool to expect a response from you. How would you do that when you live under the perception that thousands of guys are waiting for you?

What do you think of yourself? You are just an ordinary middle class and overambitious woman with thousands of limitations.

I am not a sensitive guy. I am a strong person who lives life practically but you played with my emotions. You can pretend that whatever you have done is right, and I am the one sending this crap. Try to ask yourself. You could have handled the entire chapter in a respectful manner.

The reason is that my intentions were good, but you treated me like a psycho stalker. You are going to haunt me throughout my life. You are the one who made me lose faith in life. I fear that I cannot marry anyone now. You are the first person who broke my heart. For the rest of my life, you will always be the one who hurt me the most. Don't forget that.

The emotional experience of the loss of a relationship is like experiencing death. It follows the same process as mourning a death.

Thanks for the sleepless nights, thanks for the experiences, thanks for the solitude.

Thanks a lot for the pain!

Good Bye!

Chapter 6

In my mind, I was still at the hospital. I tried to open my eyes but could not do it.

Was it the end of story between Iqbal and Rubina? I hoped not.

I wanted to stop thinking about Rubina for some time and that's when the second angel entered my life.

I was jobless again. Everything felt like a dream. I had joined the prestigious company, met a beautiful girl and on one sunny day, was sacked from the employment. I worked for six months in that firm. What did I learn in those six months?

I learned a valuable lesson that some people can misuse the policies implemented for their welfare. Did I deserve it?

Rubina could have handled it in a better way. However, there is no point crying over spilled milk. I had to focus on the future. It was a big question mark. What's next?

I narrated my side of the story to my roommates. Adding insult to injury, Bharat said, "Brother, you are crazy. We are struggling here to get a decent job, and you lost one because of some stupidity."

Harish tried to comfort me, "There is no point blaming yourself. Now you can forget and come out of her thoughts, but you have the challenge to get another job."

I said, "My biggest challenge is how will I ever convey this to my parents? They will not be able to tolerate this."

"Do not tell your parents about this now," Harish said.

"I used to send a portion of money from my salary to my mother every month. How will I manage that now?"

Harish said, "I can help you for a couple of months, in the meantime, you can try to find some small level jobs like a salesman or restaurant boy like us."

I mumbled, "Guys, things are getting complicated."

I remembered my family's visit and said, "My sister has an entrance test in Bangalore."

Harish said, "Do not worry about it."

After some time, I pulled out the envelope that the HR had given me and showed it to my friends.

"I have three months of advance salary. I may be able to survive another six months on this. I still need to find a job." The advance was like an oasis in the desert.

Harish smiled and said, "That is cool."

"Thanks a lot for your support guys."

Mom and Fouziya decided to visit me that weekend. I booked a hotel for their stay. Fouziya had a long list. She wanted to visit Wonder-la and the Innovative Film City. Then, she wanted to taste the food from Barbeque Nation, Kobe, Pizza Hut, and Dominoes.

I said to Harish, "My sister has a perfect plan to spend my three months' salary in just three days."

They both reached early in the morning. I picked them up from the railway station and checked them into a hotel. The hotel was a budget one. Fouziya's expressions were easy to read. The hotel was not the kind she was expecting.

“Tomorrow is your exam, right? Have you prepared?" I asked Fouziya to divert her attention.

“Yes, I have to revise once."

I whispered, “I have booked your return ticket for tomorrow evening."

Naturally, Fouziya did not like it, “Ikku, this is cheating… we were supposed to stay here for a week."

"There is a strike called by some Karnataka activists from this Wednesday. Also, I heard that Wonder-La's water is very dirty and you may get sick."

"Ikku, I have heard that there are some streets where we can get good *kurtis* and *salwar* materials for a reasonable price."

She continued, “Also, please take us once to a good restaurant like Kobe or Barbeque Nation."

I was trying really hard to come up with a reasonable excuse and said, “You have to travel back by bus. It will be a problem if you get an upset stomach."

That did not work at all. Fouziya counter-attacked. “If you do not want to spend the money, then just say it. We have had food from restaurants earlier as well."

I understood that she was furious. "Okay, you want to visit Barbeque Nation. Am I right? Done, I will take you there."

The next day was Monday, and I dropped Fouziya at the examination center and returned to the hotel.

"What are your office hours?" Mom asked.

That was a difficult question.

"I took a day off as you are staying alone at the hotel."

"Do not worry about me. I can manage on my own."

I never took leaves without a genuine reason since my school days. I got ready and said, "I will come in the evening.

Please call me if you need anything."

Thankfully, I had a place to go, and that was our apartment. I was lucky that she was not aware of the location.

I picked up Fouziya in the evening from her examination center.

"How was the exam?" I asked.

“I did reasonably well, but I could not manage the time efficiently.”

It is a standard reply for each student in India.

She seemed more fascinated about the city and wished to roam around Bangalore, than discuss her exam.

She said, "Ikku, could you please take a day off tomorrow?"

She continued blabbering, "Listen, I have a good plan. Early morning, we will visit MG Road and Brigade Road, and then in the afternoon we can go to Barbeque Nation as you have assured me."

"So, you did not forget about the Barbeque Nation?" I whispered.

She continued, "In the evening we can go to Bannerghatta Forest Reserve. I have heard a lot about their jungle safari.”

"What is a jungle safari?” Mom was curious.

I explained, "We will be driving in a guarded vehicle to the jungle where we can see all the animals."

According to Fouziya's plan, we were to visit MG Road in the morning. Then, I took them to Commercial Street and purchased a couple of Kurtas for her. I had already booked three seats at Barbeque Nation for 2 P.M. and then we headed towards Indira Nagar.

We found the place at the rooftop and Fouziya liked the ambience. We filled our stomachs with mouthwatering starters. With the delicious desserts, we finished our lunch.

"Ikku, tell me a good quote to update on Facebook," Fouziya said.

"I did not get you."

"Everybody updates their Facebook status whenever they visit some good restaurant," she replied promptly.

"So, do you have a Facebook account?"

"Yes, I do."

I did not encourage her, but she still uploaded a candid picture with a status message 'Having excellent time with family at Barbeque Nation, Indira Nagar'.

Fouziya was lost in her phone, and I asked her the reason.

"I am checking how many likes I have got so far for the photo that I uploaded."

She was not happy because she did not get the response that she had expected.

We came out of the restaurant. According to our plan, we were supposed to go to Bannerghatta Forest then. Bannerghatta is a little far from the city, and there was a possibility of missing the bus. Hence, we manipulated our plan a bit and decided to visit Vidhansaudha and Halasuru Lake.

Vidhanasoudha has one of the best architecture in the city. We clicked some photographs and then headed towards Halasuru Lake. When we reached the lake, it was late.

Fouziya looked at the board and said, "We still have 20 more minutes according to this board." She rushed inside.

The security guard stopped us and said, "Sorry, it is closed."

"According to the board here we still have 20 more minutes," I said.

"Sir, it takes time to ask everyone to vacate the premises."

The guard looked annoyed.

His reason was genuine, but I saw some people still getting inside.

I said, "I can still see people moving in. How can you stop only a few people from going inside?"

Mom and Fouziya looked a little fret. They were afraid that I might indulge in an argument.

I was not impressed with his answers. I said, "I am completely fine if you are fair to everybody but if you randomly stop some people from getting in, then it is not good."

That did not go down well with the security person, and he said, "Do not dare to teach me. I am aware of my duty."

"Can you give me one logical reason for not letting us get inside while allowing others?" My tone was calm and controlled.

In the meantime, a couple of people approached the security guard and inquired about the closing time.

He replied, "It is already closed."

They left without arguing. The security guard pointed at them and said, "See, how they left without saying a word? They did not show me the board like you people did."

Then he mumbled in a lower voice, "All the Muslims are the same."

I was shocked for a moment. I had never imagined that he had this in mind, that I am a Muslim, and he is Non-Muslim. I was not even dressed in a way that would tell my faith, then how did he identify me as a Muslim? Oh yes, mom was wearing a burkha and my sister was wearing a scarf.

This provoked me. "Why should my religion and faith be of any importance to you? Are there different timings for

Muslims, Hindus, and Christians?"

My voice was louder than normal and it looked like I was losing control.

"See, this is your problem," he mocked me.

I freaked out, "If you are being racist, then it is okay. If you are provoking me, then also it is fine. But if I give an explanation, then you will mock at me that I am shouting. Do you think it is fair?"

I was so furious that my mom had to drag me out of the spot.

It was not the first time that something like that had happened to me. Why couldn't everyone consider me a human being? Sometimes during coffee breaks, my colleagues asked, "Why does Islam allow a man to marry four women? Why is it so easy to get divorced from a girl by just saying the word *talaq* three times? Why do women need to wear *burqa*?

Why is there no gender equality?"

I doubt the integrity of the questioners. If they just need answers, they could easily have got it from the Internet. There are thousands of books available in the store. There are many religious intellectuals available online to whom we can ask such questions.

I get internal happiness by following the faith. I get eternal peace by praying. I try to fast during the month of Ramzan because that gives me the energy to fight the evil inside me. I never argue with anyone that 'I am right and you are wrong'.

That particular day, I might have overreacted, as I was already frustrated with my life. I lost control when someone provoked me. We returned to the hotel as it was getting late. We checked out from the hotel and I dropped them both at the bus stand.

I uploaded my resume again at all the leading job portals and waited for their response. I had more difficulty cracking interviews compared to the last time. My sudden termination from the previous company had created a negative impact on my profile.

I had two choices. Option number one was to explain the interviewers that I worked for six months with another organization. The advantage was that I could claim the training, which is valuable in the IT industry. The disadvantage was that I had to explain to them why I quit the previous organization in just six months.

My second option was to eliminate the six months of experience from my work profile and apply for another job as a fresh graduate. However, getting the job as a fresher was far more difficult. I was caught between the two stools. Finally, I decided to go ahead with the prior experience but I had to prepare an answer to tackle the interviewer's question regarding it.

What were my feelings towards Rubina now? Did I miss her? I missed her sometimes, but the intensity of the feeling was much less than the earlier times. Did I want to meet her again? I did not want to meet her again, but sometimes I stalked her Facebook page. Did I curse her? The day I quit the company, I imprecated her, but now I started thinking in both the perspectives. I wished only good things to happen in her life. But there was a possibility of running into her at public places such as malls, shopping complexes, restaurants or in the streets as we both lived in the same city. If it happens what would be her reaction?

She might act like a stranger and move on.

What was hurting more, the solitude or the rejection? At some point, we have to understand that some people stay in our heart, but not in our life. Nothing hurts more than realizing that someone meant everything to you, but you had no place in their life.

When I called my mom, she reminded me that a wedding was to happen in my immediate family. I was in a dilemma whether to attend or not. If I attended, then I would have to spend money in such a way as if I had a job. I was not in a position to spend a lot of money. I thus decided to find a reason to avoid it.

I rang Mom's number. "I cannot attend the wedding. I have to travel to Delhi due to some urgency."

She was surprised for a moment and said, “Wedding happens once in a lifetime."

"Mom, please understand. I had a software deployment, which was not successful. Now we have to travel on-site and get it fixed." I dropped the call.

I checked my e-mails. I had still not received any response from the job portal. I discussed the same with my roommates. Harish said, "There are no new vacancies as the market is down.”

Bharat said, "I am hearing this for quite some time now."

He continued, "If there is an election in the U.S., then our market is down. If there is a problem in the Middle East, then our market is down. If European Banks are in loss, then our market is down."

Harish added, "Yes, we are dependent on all other countries."

"Why are we unable to generate jobs? What is the country's biggest problem? Is the population the major issue?" The conversations lead to a debate, which continued for some time.

Bharat concluded the topic, "I don't think population is the biggest problem. If the population is the main problem, then we must have had a shortage in the agricultural sector.

The real issue is that we do not have the right skill set. For example, the government spends a major portion of the budget on Research and Development and on Defense Laboratories. After spending that huge amount, we purchase the aircrafts from other countries. We have to make India a manufacturing hub and find the market in other countries."

After a couple of days, I received the call from one of the HR executives from a company, "Am I speaking with Iqbal Abdulla?"

"This is Iqbal."

He continued, "I am calling from HCL Technologies. We have scheduled an interview for you tomorrow at 10 A.M. Can you attend it?"

I said, "Sure, I can attend it."

I was a little relieved by the call. I understood that I was following the procedures correctly.

I reached the interview location on time. The HR was a bit late and said, "Sorry for making you wait. Our technical panel is ready."

He escorted me to the room where a two member panel were present. I greeted them courteously and sat down for the interview.

In this interview, they tried testing my programming and logical skills. Then I waited outside, the HR came to me and said, "You have cleared the technical interview. Do you need a little time before the next round of interview?"

"I am ready." He took me to the HR Manager's room.

The manager asked me to introduce myself. I talked about my work experience and educational background.

As expected, his first question was, "Why was there a sudden termination from your previous employer?"

"Sir, there was a personal reason for it," I said.

He was not satisfied with the answer and started digging more. "Can you please elaborate?"

I took a deep breath and said, "I had a tussle with one of the female employees there and had to leave the company because of breach of the company policy."

He took around fifteen seconds of pause and said, "We are looking for an employee whose conduct is more sorted than the technical expertise. I am sorry to say that I cannot consider you for this job."

I said, "No problem, sir." I walked out.

I realized the stain in my work profile. Did I regret what I had done to Rubina? No, I might have done more damage if I had continued with that company. Every day was like living in hell, and I hated that place so much. That was the toughest phase of my life. I said to myself that every cloud has a silver lining.

My financial reserve was depleting quickly. The festival of *Eid Ul Fitr* was approaching. Again, I had to go home. *Eid* is a good occasion to enjoy and relax and indeed it is an occasion that causes one to spend a lot of money. I had to distribute money to all my cousins. I had to purchase clothes for my siblings and parents. I also needed to spend money on charity. According to Islamic customs, I had to spend one portion of salary to the poor as '*Zakat*'. I could not find a way to control this expense except for canceling the trip.

I did everything to cut corners.

As expected, mom was furious and shouted, "What kind of a job is it? You are unable to come home for festivals and marriages…does your manager not understand that it is an important festival for us?"

"Yes, he understands, but he is also helpless."

I disconnected the phone.

I checked my wallet and I had only 700 rupees remaining.

Something strange happened that day while I was waiting for the bus. A middle-aged person approached me and started narrating his story. "I came to Bangalore from Belgaum for passport purposes."

Long story short, he lost his wallet and mobile on the bus. He did not have any idea what to do next. I was not sure whether to help him or not. If this person was genuine, then I might regret not helping him. I offered the money that could help him reach home.

I got another interview call from a prestigious company. I conveyed upfront that I lost my previous job because of policy violation. It was no fun going through the entire interview process and returning with a heavy heart.

The HR took that positively, "I appreciate your honesty. If you qualify the technical round, I will hire you on contract basis for six months. We will monitor your activities and then absorb you to our payroll after six months. Does that sound okay?"

"Yes sir...absolutely."

I had a written exam followed by two technical interviews. I cleared all the exams and entered the HR Manager's room, "Iqbal, I assured you the job if you pass the technical interview."

After a silence, he continued, "You said that you lost the job because of policy violation. Can you explain more?"

I got some confidence as he tried to ease the communication by asking personal questions. I cleared my throat and said, "Sir, I sincerely loved a girl but, she could not understand it. She escalated the issue, went to the higher management, and I got the pink slip."

He looked cordially and said, "Do you regret that you could not get her in your life?"

"No sir, she was an angel and I was not good enough for her."

The manager had a smile on his face throughout the conversation. He said, "As I assured you, I can hire you on contract basis. If your performance and attitude is good, then we will make your employment permanent. We will conduct background verifications. But do not worry about this case. However, if you have any other incidents other than this particular case, you must leave."

"I am sure that I do not have any other incidents to tarnish my image."

"Then, no worries."

We discussed the salary. I agreed to his conditions, as I did not have other options. Then, he rolled out the offer to me.

I was so relieved and visited the Masjid. I thanked God from the bottom of my heart.

I remembered the guy who had lost his passport. Maybe he prayed for me genuinely. Sometimes, we refrain ourselves from offering help due to our life's conditions, but God always returns it in a much better way. I experienced it many times earlier. Things were getting out of my hand, and I was about to go insane. However, it helped me to become stronger and to face life in a much more practical manner.

That night, I had a sound sleep. There is nothing better than sleep. It has the power to relax the body and the mind. Sleep has the power to heal the wounds caused to the body. Sleep helps us forget the failure and humiliation caused to the heart. But, to get a good sleep, we should know the art to balance all the things in our life. I think that a person who gets regular and healthy sleep is the wealthiest person.

I did not want to remember the past and wanted to make a fresh start. I made a surprise visit to my home, and everyone was happy to meet me. I recharged myself and was ready for new challenges.

I wrote in my diary- My Dearest Past, thanks for the experiences. Future, I am ready.

Chapter 7

I woke up at 6 in the morning and stepped out after having a cup of tea. I did not forget to carry all the original documents to the new office. Unlike my previous company's first day, I did not have much anxiety this time.

There was a welcome board for the new joiners. The HR professional greeted me with a smile.

He said, “I hope you are carrying all the original documents."

I said, “Yes sir." He escorted me to the induction room.

I liked induction program for two reasons.

The first reason was, so many fun activities were conducted during the program, and the second reason was that the lunch buffet was free that day.

Administrative officials verified the documents after completion of the program, "Why is there a sudden termination from your previous employment?”

I must face this question throughout my career.

The HR Manager enrolled me to a project team after finishing the basic formalities. He handed over the contact number of the project manager.

I joined the new group. The boss, Mr. Ashok introduced

me to the team members. Senthil and Payal were a part of my team. My first impression about Senthil was that he was a cool guy. However, Payal looked a little shrewd and career oriented.

I inquired Senthil, "What is the office timing?"

He said, "Timing is not important as this is a project-based team. Try to reach 5-10 minutes before the boss reaches and leave 5-10 minutes after he leaves. So boss has the impression that you work from early morning till late at night."

Senthil continued, "I have some free advice if you have time."

"Sure." I shrugged.

He pulled his chair close to me and started, "Advice number one is that always try to make your boss happy, that helps with the survival. Advice number two is to never trust HR's assurances, for example, on-site and salary hike, and advice number three is to not expect growth in your career after you join an IT company."

In the meantime, Payal had also pulled a chair and sat next to us. She said, "Don't follow his words. He is infuriated because of waiting for the U.S. visa for the past three years."

Senthil stared at Payal and said, "My last advice, never ever trust the girls in the team."

She responded, "That is another frustration as he has had so many bad experiences."

I chuckled.

I liked Senthil. He was candid but Payal was still a mystery. I understood from Senthil that she had one year's experience, so practically she had six more months' experience than me. My speculation about Payal proved to be right when I checked the mails. She had assigned a task to me.

"FYI Iqbal, please take care of this activity."

Usually, the team leader sends these kinds of e-mails. I shared this with Senthil, and he said, "So, Payal wants to lead you, looks like she is in a hurry to climb up the ladder."

I ignored her e-mail and the next day she marked a copy of that e-mail to the boss.

Payal pulled a chair near me and inquired, "Iqbal, may I know the status of the task that I assigned to you?"

She talked like a teacher asking her students about the homework.

I said, "Sorry Payal, I could not complete it."

"May I know the reason? It should not have taken more than a day," Payal said.

I said, "Sorry Madam, I could not check my e-mail." She did not like my answer.

"I think there is a communication issue here. It is better to escalate it to the project manager," Payal said.

"Yes, that is better." I concurred.

After some time, Payal and Ashok had a private discussion. As anticipated, the boss called me into the closed session room.

Ashok initiated the discussion, "Iqbal, do you have any issues with doing the tasks?"

I cleared my throat and explained my stand, "Absolutely not, but I think that the person who allocates the tasks, should have a strong command in technology. This role demands good hands-on experience. It looks like Payal wants to lead the team, but she needs some more time to fit into that role."

Ashok tried his best not to hurt anyone's ego and said, "According to the project, it is a three member's team. Payal, Iqbal, and Senthil. All of them are equal contributors to the project, and none of them has a special role. I do not want any personal grudges in the team as that will negatively influence the project delivery."

Payal looked disconcerted after the meeting.

The next day I went to the office and greeted Payal with a smile, "Good morning".

Payal shunned me then, but after a moment she responded, "Hmmm...Morning."

It was a weird reaction. I understood that there were some underlying tuning-up issues between us.

Senthil reached office a bit late, on the way he started a communication with one of the colleagues. "Hey Ram, I called you yesterday, and you did not bother to receive the call."

Ram responded, "Oh sorry, I was in a critical position when you called."

Instead of saying 'very bad situation', Ram said 'critical position.' Senthil was quick to comment.

"Oh, I understand...newly married couple."

Ram got annoyed with the answer and said, "Hello brother, I was in the hospital."

I observed a smile on everyone's face with Senthil's presence, and it was nice to have someone like him in the team. But, the problem was that most of his jokes were below the belt.

I think Senthil had got up from the wrong side of the bed that morning.

IT Security guys came to Senthil's desk and said, "Virus alerts are coming from your computer. Please remove the network cable from your machine."

Senthil removed the cable immediately.

Support guy continued, "Please allow us to test what is causing the issue."

Senthil got up from the chair and the security team took charge. When they verified, there was a DVD in the drive. The guy opened the drive, and it was a porn movie DVD.

The security guy was astonished. "Do you know that it is a company laptop?" he said.

Senthil looked at him and said, "Sorry sir."

It was amusing. Obviously, Senthil's face at that moment was worth capturing on a camera.

After sometime, Payal came to Senthil's desk and taunted him, "How are you?"

She continued, "I don't think the boss will process your U.S. visa after this incident."

Senthil said, "Who wants a U.S. visa? There is no value for life in the U.S. People shoot each other in the street."

Payal mocked him, "Sour grapes, eh? Everyone knows how desperate you were."

Another person came to Senthil's desk and tried to poke him, "How was the movie in the DVD Drive?"

Senthil nudged him and said, "Listen, my dear friend… we all have a personal life and I also know that you sit in a corner and read movie blogs for the eight hours you spend in the office. Each year you get an A+ rating because the boss thinks that you never leave the computer and are always working."

Senthil continued and said, "I know the story of another A+ rating person. He is always online because he does stock marketing. I did not complain about all these activities and expected the same kind of gesture from the other side as well. If I secretly watch a porn movie then you make a big fuss. Do you think it is fair?"

Did I mention that Senthil is a Tamilian? It was nice to see the brotherhood between two Tamilians.

A new joiner happened to be in our group, and Senthil's first question was, "Where is your native place?"

The new joiner responded, "I am from Madurai, Tamil Nadu." On hearing this, Senthil's behavior and body language changed.

He inquired more about his background and slowly their conversation turned to Tamil. "Brother, did you have your food?"

Senthil continued, "Bangalore food is horrible macha."

I tried to poke him, "Senthil, is that your cousin?"

He said, "No."

"Family relative…?"

He said, "No dude. He is also from the same state, Tamil Nadu. Poor boy has come all the way from his hometown to work here. I was only suggesting some good places to have food."

I said sarcastically, "Does he belong to Tamil Nadu? Then, it must be too difficult for him."

There was no getting away from the frenzied assault. Senthil said "I have a particular interest towards the people of my state. What is wrong?"

I said, "Nothing is wrong. We are just jealous."

It was lunchtime and we all moved towards the canteen. On the way, Payal passed me by but ignored me completely. We were about 8-10 people, we reached the canteen. Most of them had brought lunch boxes from home. I went through the menu and ordered chicken fried rice and Coke. I took a vacant seat near Payal.

Payal stood up and settled down in the corner seat. I found that a bit uncanny. Everyone opened their lunch boxes. It was nice to see people sharing food that they had brought from home.

One of the team members, Sandeep said, "Sharing food is a good idea. It is a big relief for me."

It was a sarcastic joke, but I felt that there was some truth in it when I saw the way he enjoyed other's food.

It was fun to watch Senthil feeding the food to his newly found brother. "Macha, saappid odamb-paathukkanam." (Brother you should take care of your health.)

The discussion moved from politics to movies and then cricket. We all took a small walk after lunch and returned to work.

After some time, Senthil approached me. "Do you smoke?"

"No, I don't," I said.

"Can you at least accompany me?" That was his next question.

I said, "Sure, I can join you."

"I am getting bored here. I will also join you guys," Payal said.

We walked towards the smoking zone. There were some people smoking, including both women and men.

"This IT has spoiled the young generation. See, I never saw girls smoking before," Senthil commented.

Payal questioned him quickly, "If a man can smoke, then why can't women do the same? This is typically an Indian man's mentality," Payal muttered.

Senthil exhaled the smoke and said, "I cannot accept the lifestyle of today's youth. I can never agree on the concept of living together. At the end of the day, the girl is the one who suffers a lot. It is against our culture."

I replied, "What kind of culture it is to pass adulterous comments in front of girls? Don't you think it is double standards? I agree with Payal, why is there an uproar when a girl goes to the pub? Who are we to control girls?"

Senthil became quiet.

Payal developed a soft corner for me because I supported her views.

Payal responded, "Blaming the lady for everything is narrow-mindedness. Today's girls' want to live the way they wants because they are independent. What is wrong with that?"

Every Friday some fun activities were conducted and our boss urged everyone to participate in the them. Senthil and I joined the event.

"What is this fun activity? Is it fun?" I was curious.

"It is boring, working with excel sheets is better than this," he replied.

"We will have to answer our boss's questions if we fail to attend," Senthil muttered.

There were very few people who had gathered for the event.

Senthil said, "The company spends a lot of money on motivational programs. Instead, they can hire some good-looking girls in every team. That would be the best motivation program."

The Delivery Manager requested the Project Managers to get their respective team members. Project Managers urged the team members to participate.

Senthil said, "The Delivery Manager is having fun making our boss work."

After some time, some more people assembled and the activities began. Some games were planned with balloons, threads, and coins. Finally, there was a singing competition. Payal participated in it.

It was nice to see her on stage, and she sang a Hindi song from the movie Roja.

"I never gave it a thought earlier that Payal is so beautiful," Senthil commented.

It was true what he had said. Payal looked stunning on the stage.

A software engineer's life is incomplete without late night parties. I saw people finding reasons for celebration. They created an occasion if there was none. If someone got engaged, if someone got married, if someone had a baby, if someone got a promotion, if someone got the U.S. visa, if someone got a bonus, if someone booked a home or a car, a party was there for everything.

The IT office culture is a little different from other offices in India. I saw the highest designated person on the floor cracking jokes with a newly joined software engineer. Even for the late-night parties, there was no age, status or gender bar. Since it was Friday, everybody was in a party mood. The team was looking for someone to sponsor it.

As expected, they approached me, "Iqbal is the new joiner, and he will sponsor tonight's party."

I escaped cleverly, "I never got a welcome party from the team, so I cannot sponsor."

The team was desperately looking for an idiot to spend his money. They approached Senthil.

"Senthil, l think you were on leave last Thursday. What was the reason?"

Senthil said, "My brother was blessed with a baby."

One of the guys in the group said, "Well then that calls for a celebration. So it is decided that Senthil will sponsor tonight's party."

Senthil was in confusion. "Why should I give the party if my brother had a baby?"

"You should celebrate, as you have a new member in your family," a team member said.

Finally, all the team members convinced Senthil for the party. We decided the venue, time and the transportation facilities.

I liked the ambience of the place. It was faintly lit and perfect for drinking. We were eight people in the group and we reserved a table. All of them ordered drinks except for Payal and I. I ordered orange juice and some chicken recipe.

Our boss casually asked, "Senthil, what happened to your wedding?"

Senthil did not like the question. "Every proposal that comes to me draws more salary than me. You do not believe this. Sometimes, I cry all night, alone," he said.

Everyone started with their first peg and the mood was reticent. The discussion began with some funny incidents that had happened in the office during the week.

One of the team members, Jayant said, "Last week my wife showed me an SMS which said that an LPG Gas reimbursement was credited to the account. I said that is not gas reimbursement. That is my bonus for this year."

Everyone's mood changed and I was curious to know about Senthil's take on Jayant's comment.

Somebody poked him. "Senthil, what happened to your U.S. Visa?"

Senthil was silent for some time and then said, "I can never visit U.S. in my lifetime. Some managers give false promises to get the work done."

Everybody looked towards Ashok.

"Boss should answer this," a voice came from the corner.

"Did I guarantee you a U.S. visa? Of course, I said that I will try my best to process the visa, but it has its procedures," the boss clarified.

Senthil was not happy with the answer. Perhaps he felt that it was the right opportunity to confront the boss.

I expected drama. Senthil pulled his chair, cleared his throat and started speaking.

"I began working with this company three years ago, when the price of one cup of tea was three rupees. Now the price of the same cup of tea is six rupees, but my salary is exactly the same figure as when I had joined. Groceries and fuel these days cost an arm and a leg. After every appraisal, I am fed-up of hearing that 'You have done a good job, but we are expecting more responsibility as you are a senior team member.' If you expect more responsibility from me, then how can you say that I have done a good job? Don't you think this statement is contradictory?"

There was silence for a moment, and he continued, "My situation is like sugarcane, in the first-year the company extracted all the juices inside me. The second year, I stretched myself to produce some more juice. Even after I had given my best performance, I did not get the recognition that I deserved. I do not have any juice remaining to produce now."

Senthil was not in a mood to stop, "In all these years, the only thing that has improved is 'the dependency'. I was not allowed to take holidays during Diwali, Ganesh Chaturthi, or Pongal because there were either production issues or critical deployments. I have seen your e-mail where you explained the policies implemented for the welfare of the employees. If the company wants to do something for the employees then it should allow employees to take leaves during the festival time."

Senthil was taking out all the frustration that had been burning inside him. He looked closely at the manager and said, "Also while sending the revised salary, please avoid the text, 'it is confidential and do not show to others'. I am equally ashamed myself to show it to others."

Senthil concluded and said, "You cannot fool this generation easily, we are smart. We can read the silence between the words."

As expected, Ashok was not happy the way Senthil had asked questions. He managed the erupting chaos quite well. "Senthil, please rectify your mistakes before pointing to someone else. How can I recommend a person whose laptop is full of porn movies? Do you think nobody is aware of this? Try to improve yourself and then demand from the management. If you have complaints, we can have a one to one discussion. This is not the right platform."

That is how Ashok closed Senthil's mouth and that proved the universal truth that the boss is always smarter. Another team member whispered, "Senthil asked genuine questions but the place and the timing were inappropriate."

Everybody had finished their drinks by then and we ordered the main course. I went to the restroom and while returning, I saw Payal standing alone at the balcony.

"Why are you here?" I asked.

She said, "I do not like parties. Most of the times, I try to avoid coming here. Today I could not do it."

I noticed one of our team members vomiting badly.

I said, "I do not understand why people drink so much. My roommates get severe headaches the day after their drinking sessions."

We all finished our dinner and departed. Most of them hired a cab to reach home.

Chapter 8

I was happy to experience the office life again. It was Monday morning.

Senthil reached office a little late.

"How are you Senthil?" Payal asked.

"I am doing great. Do you know who the most cunning creatures in this world are?"

Payal did not answer. Senthil continued, "Project Managers."

"I hope I did not go overboard that day. I just couldn't control venting out my frustration. In fact, I was looking for an opportunity to attack Ashok," Senthil continued without stopping to take a breath.

Payal said, "You are lucky, he is on leave today."

"Oh, that is cool." Senthil turned on his laptop.

I do not generally crack jokes on adultery in the presence of female colleagues but others in the office did that quite often.

In UNIX technology, a few processes run overnight. The processes are to facilitate data transferring from one server to another, so the knowledge about its technical details were not required. These processes were also called "Job".

In the team, there was a newly married guy called Jagdeesh.

Senthil once asked him loudly, “Jagdish, how was last night’s job?”

Jagadeesh understood the sexual undertone to Senthil’s question but chose to reply sensibly.

"Yes Senthil, it had run."

Senthil continued, "Was it successful?”

"Yes, it was successful."

Senthil was unstoppable, he said, "If it is not successful, schedule it in the morning."

I observed that the office environment was completely different whenever the boss was on leave. I could recall that it was similar to the school days when we would go wild whenever our class teacher was absent. Nobody bothered about work.

Payal left the office a bit early.

"Sorry to bother you, Iqbal...Are you still in the office?” Payal was a little hesitant. Probably she wanted some help.

"Yes, I am."

She continued, "There are a pair of spectacles in my drawer, could you please keep it with you?"

"Sure, but I have never seen you wearing specs.”

"I generally use contact lenses but keep spectacles for backup. I forgot them in the office today.”

"Okay. I can hand them over to you at your home. Please send me your address."

I borrowed a bike to drop the spectacle box at Payal’s residence.

She was ecstatic to see me and said, “It would have been so difficult without these. I wake up many times in the night.

Thanks a ton."

The following day, Payal greeted me with a delightful smile.

"How are you?"

"I am doing well." This was the first time that she had greeted me.

"Usually, I am not that forgetful."

"Why can't you sleep with the contact lenses on?" I was curious.

"Because if the lenses are worn overnight, they leave a burning sensation in the eyes," Payal explained.

"Then you should keep a spare one along with you at all times."

She nodded in agreement.

She checked her e-mails and said, "Senthil is on sick leave today."

"I think he is avoiding the Manager."

It was around 12:00 P.M. Payal whispered, "Shall we go for lunch? I am already starving."

"I think the team will take lunch at 1 P.M."

After thinking for a moment, I said, "Sure, we can go."

She had brought home cooked lunch.

"Do you cook?" I was curious.

"Yes, not by choice though…I don't put up with my family, I live with my friends."

"Where are you from?" I thought of using the standard question of driving the conversation to a personal level.

"I am from Rajasthan but I am quite familiar with this city. I completed my graduation here in Bangalore itself."

She opened her lunch. It was veg fried rice and two

different desserts.

“It smells of home."

“Obviously, I prepared it at home," she said with a smile.

I started probing deep into her family details and she said,

"My father is a businessman. My mom is a homemaker and I am their only daughter."

She offered me *gajar ka halwa.*

"This *halwa* is awesome. I can join you for lunch daily if you promise to offer me such delicious desserts."

She giggled and said, "Of course."

"I like sweets, and my options are limited because I am a vegetarian," she grinned.

“Oh, that's wonderful. I dearly respect vegetarian people. But I can never imagine myself becoming a vegetarian even in my wildest dreams."

I felt a little dozy after lunch. I was so full.

I said, "I am feeling sleepy now."

"I am also feeling the same. Do you like to play carrom?"

"I can play, but I am not a pro at it."

We sat to play a round and she beat me badly within a few minutes. We then moved to the table tennis court.

I asked, "Do you play table tennis?"

“No, I can learn if you teach me."

I explained the rules to her and the basic steps, and then in order to motivate her, I said, "Payal, you are a quick learner."

I had complimented only to make her feel good about herself but she thought I was observing her game intently.

"Everybody tells me that I catch on quick."

I chose not to comment anything on her exceptional

quality. I slowly grew accustomed to this tentative but pleasant companionship.

I had made a huge blunder that day. I removed one of the important folders while going through the module code. It was indeed a critical mistake. A ticket was raised and all the teams started working to solve the problem.

Our manager got the intimation and rushed to our desk. He asked what the issue was.

I started explaining but Payal interrupted me and said, "Ashok, I was working on a production issue and I removed the folder by mistake."

Ashok asked in astonishment, "Payal, do you even understand the significance of it?"

The atmosphere in the office changed completely. There were conference calls happening after almost every five minutes, as we had to keep the seniors updated.

A group of managers from Contra-Distinct team approached us.

Ashok rushed towards Payal and said, "There is a call from the location head, please give me the status."

She answered annoyed, "Either I can answer the phone calls or try to fix this issue, I cannot do both."

The boss tried to calm her down, “Okay, you please take care of this issue and I will tackle this call.”

She finally found the backup file from the preceding month's deployment and uploaded the folder. Fortunately, the issue was soon fixed.

"Good work that you fixed this on priority. But, be careful in the future," said Ashok.

After everybody left, I asked Payal, “Why did you save me?”

She said, "It is important that you do not screw up your

first impression. It is even more important to be alert at all times for someone who is a new member in the team."

It was Friday evening.

"Shall we plan a trek for this weekend?" That was Senthil's voice.

I found that interesting, and said, "Yes, it is a good idea, but we need someone good at trekking to accompany us."

Senthil responded, "Do not worry, I have good experience."

Payal interrupted, "Do you think we are fools here to accompany you?"

I surfed the internet to look for a nice hill station for trekking and said, "This one is not at a high altitude, we can go trekking here without a trainer.

Senthil, Payal, Payal's friend, Ritika and I were part of the plan.

Senthil pretended to be a highly-trained trekker.

"Guys, it is imperative that we start trekking before the sun rises high in the sky. We should reach the spot at 6 in the morning. Everyone should be ready with their trekking shoes and jackets."

He thought something for a minute and then asked us all, "Any questions?" Payal could not stop laughing looking at his body language and composure.

It was 6 in the morning. Everyone reached the location, except Senthil.

Payal said, "I know that he will make us wait for him."

I called his number, and he received the phone call. I understood that he was still asleep, but he promised me that he would reach as soon as possible.

We waited for almost an hour before he reached.

“Sorry guys, there was heavy traffic. That’s why I could not make it on time.”

Payal asked, "Heavy traffic? Really? It is still too early for your excuse to be justified. Why are you fooling yourself?”

I said, "There is no point in wasting any more time, we should begin with our trip."

Senthil did not forget to add, “Guys, please let me know if you need any help."

We ignored him.

Senthil’s exemplary comic sense is the thing that makes us forget and forgive his mistakes. That particular day, Payal seemed a little different to me. The way she looked beautiful in her western clothes and especially her jacket. I observed keenly, the way she fixed her headphones.

The cloudy weather made it an ideal day for trekking. The monsoons had spread greenery all around. A light breeze blew that had the magic to bring about nostalgic feelings.

We had trekked almost halfway, when we looked down and were mesmerized by the beauty of God’s creation. "This is the best place to visit with someone special," Senthil said.

I observed that Senthil was trying hard to impress Ritika, the new girl in the group.

"I love adventure. I never miss an opportunity for trekking or other adventurous games,” Senthil boasted.

Ritika did not give him much attention, but Senthil continued with his mission and said, "I suggested going to Savandurga hill station, this place is actually for kids."

Payal whispered in my ears, “This guy is crossing the limit. Let us play a prank on him.”

Payal shouted loudly that she had seen a snake crawling behind Senthil. It was amusing to watch Senthil as he was terrified.

Payal said, "I have to salute Senthil's spirit. I have never seen him lose confidence."

We all rested for a while under a banyan tree and had breakfast together.

Senthil gazed at me and asked, "Do you have a girlfriend?"

I was little surprised as it was an unexpected question.

"No, I don't. I haven't been that lucky," I replied.

I thought it was a fascinating subject to discuss, as I was keen to know Payal's status. However, I felt it was not right to ask her directly as she could misunderstand me.

I started with Senthil, "What about you Senthil?"

He responded, "It is a sad story."

Payal responded promptly, "Let us hear about that story some other day."

I encouraged him, "Please go on. We are ready to listen."

He began speaking, "I was in a relationship with a beautiful girl in our town but could not marry her as we belonged to different religions. One fine day, we decided to elope. I requested my best friend to pick her up and I waited for her in the car. I waited until my watch ticked midnight but none of them came. I called my friend and when my calls went unanswered, I realized that they both had run away together."

He took a deep breath and then said, "I realized it later that they both were just using me."

I could not stop laughing and said, "That is an interesting story if it is true."

Then, I looked at Ritika, "How about you? Do you have a boyfriend?"

She said, "Well, I have a friend, and we are going to get engaged very soon."

Senthil was overcome by sadness and it showed on his face.

I was sure that he was asking God why he was cruel to him.

Finally, I turned towards Payal, "What about you Payal?"

She said, "Oh, me? No...I could never find a suitable guy."

"According to you, what are the qualities of a suitable guy?" Senthil was quick to ask.

She said, "Well, my suitable guy should be exactly the opposite of you."

Senthil said, "Come on guys, let us continue."

Senthil and Ritika continued the trek. Payal and I stayed back and she looked at me and said, "Since I consider you my good friend, I would like to share something really important with you."

I said, "Of course, you can trust me."

She stammered a bit, "Well...I have some personal issues."

She kept quiet for some time and then continued, "I had a serious relationship with a guy, I regretted being with him, even when I knew him well. I want to end the relationship completely but he is harassing me mentally and physically.

I said, "I understand your situation. Do you want some help?"

She said, "I could not even share it with my parents as they would get concerned. I consider you as my good friend and someone whom I can trust completely."

I looked into her eyes and said, "Thank you for trusting me, you can approach me for any help."

I felt a little lost after listening to her heartbreaking experience.

Was I relieved that she was not dating anyone? Why did

her being single matter to me so much? Three months ago, I was so much in love with Rubina that I could not imagine being with any other girl, but now I had started liking Payal's presence. I wanted to know more about her, talking to her made me happy. I had also grown a little possessive about her. Was it love? I was not even sure what Payal thought about me.

Was it something else that haunted me?

It started to drizzle as we were about to leave.

I said, "The beauty of hill stations is that rains are so unpredictable here."

The breeze after the rains appealed to my senses.

Payal untied her hair, she looked stunning and the weather enhanced her gorgeousness. She pulled out an umbrella from her bag and opened it.

She said, "Come under the umbrella."

At first, I was a little reluctant to go but then I sensed that it might start raining heavily. Finally, we were both under one umbrella.

"Oh, it's so chilly here," Payal said.

The umbrella was a really small one and Payal stood very close to me. It felt enchanting to observe her expressions so closely. I could feel her breathing. During monsoons, I never forget to carry an umbrella with me but on that day, I was fortunate to forget.

After the rain stopped, we continued our trek. It was still a long journey to reach the peak of the mountain. A few meters of walk exhausted Payal completely. We still had to walk more and the path ahead was not an easy one.

"Will you be able to climb without a rope?" I asked her.

"No, I don't think so."

I took out a rope from my bag and fixed it into one of the

trees.

I said, "You can carry on."

She tried to balance and climb, but in vain.

I suggested, "You can hold my arm if that helps."

She said, "Okay, sure...we can try that."

She held my arm tightly and tried to move further.

Her touch on my arm brought shivers to my body. I was thrilled to help someone for the first time in my life.

It was an amazing feeling. I was climbing with a girl clinging on to me but it felt as if she was a weightless feather.

Payal had a tough time balancing. She lost control a couple of times. This one time, she lost her grip and fell over my shoulder. I said, "If I lose the grip, we both will fall."

"I know that you will not let me fall. I am safe with you."

Finally, we reached the hill. We met Senthil and Ritika there.

"How did you manage trekking in this rain?" I was curious.

Senthil answered, "We used a huge tree as shelter, where I narrated my college stories to Ritika. I hope she enjoyed them."

She whispered, "I have never experienced such rain in my lifetime."

I said, "Come on guys, let us continue."

After 2-3 hours of struggle, we reached the peak. Although it was a small hill station, it felt like a massive achievement.

Little achievements in our daily lives help us regain our energy and renew our souls. The things we consider little have the power to majorly influence our lives, like getting up early in the morning, going for a jog, playing with kids, listening to old melodious songs, reading autobiographies and traveling to new places. All of these things subconsciously stimulate our minds. The reality is that in the hustle bustle of life, we are unable to find time for ourselves, to unwind and replenish our minds.

I remember very well the words of my old manager, "I am a 55-year-old man. My only regret in life is that I was not able to spend any quality time with my wife and children."

This made me realize that generally, the companies treat their efficient employees as valuable assets but my employer took just three hours to sack me. Therefore, it is important to find time to live a little, to breathe in the open air and experience life beyond cubicles.

We had lunch and goofed around for some time. After a couple of hours, we were ready to leave for home.

I felt something unusual in Payal's goodbye to me. It sounded a little personal.

It felt like she was going to miss me. I boarded the bus and occupied the window seat. I waved at her, she was still waiting for her bus.

I felt happy for the first time in so many months. I was totally lost in my world of trance.

I played all the beautiful memories of the trip in my mind over and over again. Payal's words echoed in my ears-'I know that you will not let me fall. I am safe with you'.

I talked to my heart that this was just the beginning of my love story. Will Payal help me complete it? Can I win the heart of my girl? Oh God, please have some mercy, show me a way.

I wished that day had more hours. I reached home dog-tired. I took a shower and had my dinner. I slipped into a deep and relaxing sleep. Strangely, even my dreams were in sync with the events that had happened in my waking life. Early morning, the doorbell rang but I was still dreaming of Payal's phone call. I brushed my teeth and went to a restaurant for breakfast. I was late and there was nothing to eat. I requested for a tea and while waiting for them to prepare it, my thoughts wandered to Payal again. I wondered what she would be doing. I wondered if she missed me too.

I was about to dial her number when I saw an incoming call from Payal flashing on my screen. I got confused for a second.

"Hello, how are you?" Payal's asked in the sweetest tone.

I said, "I am exhausted."

"Same here, I am so bored and feeling lazy."

"What is your plan for today?"

I said, "I do not have a specific plan. I will sleep if nobody disturbs me."

"Okay, then I will disturb you. Will you go out with me this evening?"

I said, "Sure, where do you want to go?"

She took a moment to decide the venue and said, "I hope you won't mind if we go to a coffee shop?" She hung up the call and messaged me the address.

I wore black jeans and a glossy blue T-shirt. I showered nicely and borrowed a perfume and cream from Harish. I was ready before time. I still had 3 hours in my hands. I watched T.V., read the newspaper, but nothing interested me. I listened to music for some time and then left for the date. I reached the coffee house but still had one more hour to while away.

It was a beautiful coffee shop situated near the lake. Payal arrived fifteen minutes late.

She said, "Hi Iqbal."

I greeted her and then gawked at her.

She sat down and said, "I hope I am not late."

"No, no...you are on time."

She looked at the menu and asked, "What will you order?"

I had a glance at the menu and ordered an espresso, whereas she ordered a cappuccino. We began the conversation and talked non-stop for more than two hours about everything under the sun.

I asked, "Shall we order some more?"

She said in her sweet voice, "Sure."

I was glad to know that she liked me too. We had so much in common, our conversation was genuine and flowed like water.

A new flower had unexpectedly sprouted in the garden of my life. I closely looked into her eyes and then stared at her hair, her nose and then my gaze shifted to her lips. My attraction towards her had grown multiple times since the first time I saw her. At first, she was a normal girl but now I found her pretty in whatever she wore. I felt like I was getting closer to her with each passing day, but I still did not know what she thought of me.

Subconsciously, I was comparing our date with my date with Rubina. For any relationship to work, it is important that the girl and the boy both should have an accepting nature. Otherwise, it doesn't matter how much we try to impress the other person, we will always end up making a fool of ourselves.

I think, the pain afflicted by a girl can never be healed with alcohol or books, but only by another girl.

It is a wrong perception that true love happens only once in a lifetime. However, I agree that there is a difference between the first love and the second one. I was crazy after Rubina but I became a more mature person with my second love.

I said, “My friend lent me his bike and I promised him that I would return it within an hour.”

“Okay then, let’s make a move,” she said.

I paid the bill and we walked towards the bike. I could read it in her eyes that she wanted to spend some more time with me. I kick-started the motorcycle.

She settled down in the back seat, tried to balance herself, and asked, "Where can I hold you?"

I said, “You can hold my shoulder."

She said, "It is alright."

She put her hand on my shoulder. It was the first time that a pretty girl was with me on a bike.

I said, "It is a nice street to walk, shall we park the bike here and go for a walk?”

"Sure."

After a small walk, I insisted to drop her home, and she obliged.

Chapter 9

Those were the wonderful days of my life. It is a beautiful feeling when we have someone to care for us. I was not sure if I was missing this care because I was away from home. Maybe earlier I had knocked the wrong door in my subconscious search for love and care.

During the office days, Payal helped me with all the tasks and assignments, in the afternoon we had lunch together which she carried from home. We also spent some quality time in the food court after the work.

Usually, we both stayed in the office until late. Even after reaching home, we were engaged on the phone until midnight. We talked about anything and everything. This gave me a feeling of a protective and secure layer around me. Payal loved me a lot and she was ready to do anything for my happiness, and even I did the same for her. Her love and care is not easy to put in words.

One evening, I was out partying and texted Payal, "I will be late tonight."

I requested her to sleep and not to wait for my call, but she insisted that I inform her, when I reach home.

It was almost two in the night when I reached home and

decided not to disturb her sleep. To be on a safer side, I dropped a message instead of calling.

Instantly I received a reply from Payal. I said, “I am so happy that you were waiting for me for so long.”

We talked for some more time and then slept. These little things help us realize that how much someone loves us. Those were the days, when we both used to wait for weekends. We watched movies, tried new places to eat and did adventures together. I was fed up of borrowing the bike from friends thus purchased a brand new Black Pulsar.

I always liked this bike since my college days. I headed towards Payal's house as soon as I purchased the bike.

"Liked it?”

I understood from her expressions that she liked it. She said, “Yes, I love it. I am so happy that you came all the way to show it to me.”

We shared all the happy moments together and genuinely felt that she was my well-wisher. I requested Payal to take the backseat, as we were to go for a long ride. We were riding on the new Airport Road and were miles away from the main city.

A brand-new bike, beautiful girl and no traffic, I was on cloud nine. I accelerated the bike and Payal held me tightly. I felt good when she embraced me that way, I did not need the jacket to cover myself. I used to feel that I had Payal to guard me against everything and I was safe in her embrace.

We reached Nandi Hills after riding around 60 kilometers. It was noon but the weather was pleasant. I sat on a bench and Payal took a seat beside me. She observed each and everything around. Another couple was sitting near us. Payal pointed out three things that amazed her. First, she said, “That lady is blessed with luscious hair but hasn't maintained it properly.”

She looked around and then said again, “She is wearing those bangles, and they don’t even match her outfit.”

She noticed one more thing and said, “That guy is wearing sports shoes with formals. It is so odd.”

Payal then looked at me and said, “Do you know something? South Indians don’t have fashion sense at all. They wear shoes with lungi and ride bikes. Only God knows that how do they balance. Payal’s comment upset me because I am a South Indian myself. I said, “I think we are way better at cleanliness even if we are lagging behind in fashion.”

I continued after a moment, “I visited Agra last year. I used a public toilet and it was horrible. I am sure that you will never find such toilets in South India. You will find cleanliness even if you go to ordinary restaurants there.”

Obviously, she did not like my counter attack. She said, “What is the use of keeping the restaurant clean? You people serve the same old food, since early morning. There is always a board hanging in the restaurant saying ‘Meals Ready’. The eating style is horrible too. They mix rice, *sāmbhar*, curd, and *rasam*, and then have it as if they have not eaten in ages.”

Her reaction irked me and I responded politely, “We South Indians prefer comfort over fashion. We do not bother what others think of us. We eat how we like and wear what suits us. We live for ourselves and not for others.”

She did not say anything, so I continued, “Do you know the fact that South India leads with good institutions and companies. All the North Indians come here for IT jobs. Forget about IT jobs, even for daily wages, people from states like Bihar, Uttar Pradesh, and Bengal move to Kerala.”

She said, "I do not agree with you. Migration for jobs happens across India and not only from North to South."

I said, “Let me tell you something that we both will agree

upon. The only thing that is common across the North and South India is the women abuse. Females are raped all across the country and victims are not just the young women. From a three-year-old girl to a 70-year-old woman, all are abused. According to a Government report, a rape happens every 20 minutes in India."

There was a silence for some time and then Payal said,

"Yes, that is the sad truth."

We reached a deserted area. I was craving for such an opportunity. I had suppressed all such feelings to let Payal feel comfortable around me. I wanted to be a good guy but I couldn't resist and gently pulled her into my arms and she surrendered. I then hugged her tightly and locked her into my chest. She tightened the grip and slowly pushed her against the wall. The distance between our lips was even less than an inch. I tried to kiss her a couple of times but she resisted and looked away.

I softly kissed her lips. I was flying as it was the first time I had kissed a girl. I said, "This is awesome."

There is no end to a man's desire. After kissing, my hands tried to feel her but she pushed me away. It was a fantastic experience but it lasted only for a couple of seconds.

"What happened to you?" It was confusing to me.

She replied, "Nothing, let us please go home."

On our way back home, we did not speak at all and I saw tears in her eyes.

The next day, it was my birthday and Payal wanted me to take a day off from work to spend time with her. I did not like the idea and said, "I am not a kid anymore to take a leave for celebrating my birthday."

She said, "You never know what will happen in future if we will be together on your next birthday or not."

"Why do you say that?" It was surprising to me.

She settled down and said, "Do you think your parents will give their consent for our marriage?"

After a moment, I said, "No, they won't accept."

There was a painful silence and I then broke the ice and said, "It is very complicated. You know the problems in a Muslim guy marrying a Hindu girl. It is not something that impacts our dependents also as we are part of the society."

In that moment of stillness, we did not know how to offer solace to each other.

"Will you marry me against your family's wish?" I was curious to know her answer.

She responded promptly, "That question does not arise as you already explained your stand."

I asked her again, "Will you marry me against your family's wish?"

She answered this time, "My situation is very similar to yours, but my parents have never forced me into anything. They won't be able to accept you wholeheartedly but I feel they will surrender for my happiness."

I did not know what to say.

She continued, "Forget everything and let us celebrate your birthday."

It was my 24th birthday. At exactly 12 o' clock, my roommates gifted me a bouquet with a note on it that said- Many many happy returns of the day my sweetheart.

Harish said, "This is from Payal and a very happy birthday to you brother."

"Thanks, man," I said and took the bouquet from him.

In the meantime, Payal called me up and wished.

I said, "Thanks for the flowers. It is all new to me."

We talked for some time and before hanging up she said,

"I would like to have breakfast together with you, be ready by 9."

It was my first birthday when I had taken off from work. I picked Payal and we went to the Park. It had a nice spot where we could silently sit and enjoy the food.

She said, "I have made breakfast for you."

She opened the box, it was *dosa* and *idly*.

"Oh, you prepared South Indian dishes."

She responded. "This is the first time I have made *dosa*. I am not sure whether you will like it."

I tasted, and it was superb. "This is awesome."

We finished our breakfast, and I asked casually, "What is the plan?"

"We are going to Central Mall."

I drove my bike towards MG Road.

"What is the next surprise?" I shrugged and smiled.

She said, "I have planned many things but promise me that you won't say no to anything."

I responded, "I am not going to deny anything, but please do not expect the same on your birthday."

She rebutted my comment and said, "I am not doing all this with any expectations. You still do not know me very well."

I tried to cover-up and in my defense, I said, "Hey, it was a joke. Only God can understand girls…no offense to God or girls."

She smiled, and we entered the mall.

I saw Payal exploring the collection of all the expensive brands.

I said, “I won’t deny anything on one condition. Please don’t buy anything expensive for me.”

I took her to the John Players store and purchased a light blue shirt and black jeans.

After the lunch, Payal said, "We are going to watch a movie in PVR. Also, I have planned a dinner in a nice restaurant."

I said, "Why are you so kind to me? We are not even sure about our future...I will be so hurt if I lose you. The higher you climb, the harder you fall."

She held my hand and said, "Forget about tomorrow and let us just live in the present. Destiny has brought us together, so let us leave everything to destiny."

We had lunch and watched the movie.

She said, "I have reserved a table at the Hilltop restaurant for 8 pm. We still have two more hours, what do you want to do until then?”

I did not need anything else to keep me busy when I was with Payal. We reached the restaurant at the scheduled time and waited for our table. The restaurant was on top of a hill, it had a mesmerizing view of the city.

I looked below and everyone seemed so tiny, mechanically rushing to reach home after office. Sometimes I regret moving to the city. We needed to be at the top of a hill or a botanical garden to get some fresh air. People say that cities give us a better life but they do not realize that they are compromising on the quality of life. We got our table, and we entered the hall. I liked the ambience.

I said, "Oh, this is a candlelight dinner."

The waiter came with a cake. Payal whispered, "I ordered a small cake."

"It's not a small cake, how will we finish it?”

She said, "Do not worry about it. We can get it packed for

take away."

Handing me the menu, Payal said, "Here is the menu for non-vegetarian items."

"Today I will only eat vegetarian food. I don't know how will I ever repay for all the surprises you planned for me. I can at least do this."

"Thank you. It is good for your health too."

The waiter served the dishes and I recalled Payal's comments about the table manners of South Indian people and began eating with spoon and fork.

She stared at me for some time, then chuckled and said, "You please eat comfortably."

I was still determined to finish the food with the spoon.

After dinner, I dropped her home and conveyed to her all that I had in my heart. I said, "This is the most beautiful day of my life and I will never forget it in this lifetime."

The next day, we had some hilarious moments during the conference call. We had a meeting with clients to discuss the weekly status. Our clients were from the US and Senthil had some difficulty understanding the accent. John, our stakeholder from the US, explained the process but Senthil could not follow. John asked about the project timeline and the delivery date, "What is the time frame for the project?"

Senthil looked perplexed by John's question, and then he tried to cover-up, "Yes, Yes..."

Boss interrupted, "Senthil! That question was for you."

John repeated the question. "What is the time-frame that we have?"

Senthil only understood one word, 'Time' and said, "John, the time in India is 5:30 pm."

After the meeting, I met Payal. She seemed gloomy. I

asked her, “What happened?”

She replied, "I want to speak something with you. Shall we go to the food court?"

I said, "Give me 10 minutes and I will join you."

We both reached the food court.

I bought tea for us. "What happened? Your parents got any new proposals?” I was anxious to know the reason for her sadness.

"No, Last night Vishal called me, and we had a long argument."

I understood whom she was referring to. Vishal was obviously her ex-boyfriend. I did not say anything and allowed her to vent. She said, “He had passwords of all my personal email IDs. He accessed my emails and checked my mobile bill reports.”

I shot a question at her anxiously, “Do you need to hide anything from anyone?"

She did not answer this question, but tried to explain her point, "Iqbal, you do not know anything about Vishal. He is a psycho.”

She took a long pause and then continued, “You know what...Vishal is a cocaine addict. During our relationship, he abused me physically and mentally. I am not someone who breaks the relationship without a strong reason. I could not bear his antics and finally called off. But he is my distant relative and he knows my parents and other relatives very well.”

“Why is he troubling you if you have broken up with him?” I was confused.

"He still needs me, and I am the one who broke up with him. So, he naturally has a problem with that.”

We both quietly sat for some time, and then Payal

continued, "I am terrified. He can do anything. I tried explaining that we are only friends but some of my emails explicitly reveal that we are more than just friends."

She gazed at me and then continued speaking. "He humiliated and insulted your religion. He said that he will inform some Hindu extremist group and then they will take care of everything."

I could not stop laughing and said, "We are living in a democratic country. We can go to any police station or even the court. Do not worry about me."

"What if he informs your family?" I was curious to know her response.

After thinking for some time, she said, "I know about my parents, they trust me a lot."

I said, "Since he is your relative, he can even go to the limits of creating problems regarding your marriage proposals."

She said, "It hardly matters to me."

"Why so?"

She responded, "I don't feel like getting married."

She was still upset and confused. I could do nothing to make her feel better.

"Is there any chance that we both can get married?" I looked at her innocent eyes when she asked this.

Payal already knew the answer to this question but she needed some hope so that she could feel a little better.

She continued. "I am sorry. I will not take you away from your family. But, will you be able to forget me easily?"

I said, "This is the happiest time of my life, and I will never be able to forget it in this lifetime."

She smiled with tears in her eyes and said, "Thank you so much."

I said, "As you said earlier, let us leave that to God, and he will show us a way."

“May I ask something? I hope you won’t mind?” I asked casually.

She looked at me confusingly. “How did you fall into the trap of such a guy?” I asked.

She gave me a prompt reply, “This is something I want to erase from my memory permanently. I know him since I was in 9th standard. He was like a close family member and often visited our home. I later realized that he came to see me. Initially, we talked over messages and then went on to chatting on social networking sites. After some days, we began talking over the phone.”

I interrupted her. “You said that he is your relative, and then you must be knowing about him already?”

She was very quick to answer my question.

“Everybody makes mistakes when they are young. It is difficult to make the right decision at the tender age of 14 or 15. He was showering me with so much love and care. I thought that his behavior would change with time. It was only later that I understood his reality and by then I had already gotten too close to him.”

I said, "You should end everything with him. Do not let him contact you. That is the only way you can have peace of mind.”

I continued, “Listen, pick your phone and call him right now. Make the conversation short and convey a clear message. Can you do that?"

"I can do that...but I am worried about the consequences," she stammered.

“He can do nothing. He is trying to take advantage of your innocence."

I continued, "I do not want to force you but, you will not have peace of mind if you do not close this matter."

She finally agreed and said, "You are right. I will close this matter right now." She grabbed the phone from her handbag and started to dial Vishal's number.

She put the call on speaker. Vishal received the call after a couple of rings.

She said, "Vishal, I want to speak about something with you."

Vishal did not say anything and Payal continued, "I tried my best to make our relationship work but unfortunately, it did not work. I want to end everything and don't want us to talk again. Please do not trouble me either on the phone or on emails. I am going to block your number and IDs."

Vishal said, "Looks like someone is helping you with all this. You are going to regret it Payal."

She gave a blunt reply to Vishal's threat and said, "Fuck off!"

Payal disconnected the call and took a deep breath.

"Do you feel better now?"

"Yes, my heart feels lighter now, and I do not want to think anything about him."

After some days, Payal was completely over him. She started getting irritated at small things. If I did not receive her call on time, she fought with me. Perhaps she was feeling insecure.

It would get extremely difficult to convince her that I missed her phone calls due to some important work. The conversation usually started this way, "Do you know something? You do not care for me at all but I care for you so much. How can you be so rude to me? Don't you know that I am not able to sleep without talking to you?"

It did not end there, "We are not going to get married, and that is the reason you do not want to get too close."

She was very conscious, and even little ignorance from my side created so much trouble for her. None of my answers satisfied her. Probably she could not digest the truth that we were bound to separate someday.

One Saturday, my roommates were off to their hometowns and I was alone in the apartment.

I requested Payal, "Can you please come to my house?"

Initially, she said no but after some pleading, she agreed.

As expected, she uncannily looked at the miserable condition of my room. She took a broom and began sweeping. Payal said, "You will fall sick if you do not maintain cleanliness."

"Shall I make anything for you?" She requested.

"I can go out and get vegetables if you feel like cooking."

"Yes, I want to cook something for you," Payal said excitedly.

She prepared *pulav* and *gajar ka halwa*.

I said, "Now I understand the logic behind marriage."

After lunch, we watched TV together. Payal sat near me and was so close to me that her shoulder rubbed against mine. I held her hand and she liked that and started to play with my fingers.

I said, "Your hands are softer than mine."

"My heart is also softer than yours," she joked.

I muttered, "That's true," and kissed her forehead.

I wanted to kiss her chin. I firmly embraced her and began kissing her face. I slowly moved to her lips. That was a beautiful moment of anticipation. She did not resist and I leaned in.

Finally, we had the perfect kiss. She closed her eyes and we were lost in each other. The last time I kissed her, she was uncomfortable as we were out in an open area.

"Why do you close your eyes?" I asked.

She responded, "Beautiful things in life are meant to be felt only by the heart."

"I don't know, I feel like holding your hands, being together all the time. But I also feel guilty." The truth was that we both were unable to control our sexual desires.

We were sitting on a sofa cum bed. I did not want to stop even when my mind resisted. I kissed her hair and bit her ears tenderly. She was aroused and started biting my lips and chin. I hugged her tightly and could feel her breasts against my body.

I wanted to feel her up as she had a beautiful body and my hands started to wander. All of a sudden, she stood up and said, "Iqbal, let us not do that."

I looked at her in confusion.

She said, "We are not even sure about our future. I don't want us to regret later"

She repeated the same thing. "Iqbal, let us not do that."

I did not say anything, and she understood my agreement to her request in my silence. Sometimes silence speaks a thousand words.

She looked at the clock and said, "It is getting late."

I did not want her to leave and she read it in my eyes.

She kissed my lips and then on my eyes. I understood all that she wanted to convey through those kisses.

She said, "I might have done something dreadful, and that is the reason I cannot have you in my life."

"You are the nicest person I know."

She was in a hurry to leave and said, "Can you please drop me at my place."

I hugged her and then dropped her home.

After returning home, I checked my mobile inbox, and there was a message from Payal.

"What do you think? Don't I have the desire? You are the sole reason for my happiness. You are the wind beneath my wings. I really cannot imagine losing you."

Chapter 10

On a misty evening, I was busy sipping coffee with Payal and she said, “My Papa is coming to Bangalore for the weekend."

“Should I tell him about our relationship?” Payal asked me.

I asked, "Do you think it is a good idea?"

“I think it would be better if someone elder from our families supported us.”

I did not answer.

"Shall we just try? Please...”

She continued, “I know my Papa, he will do anything for my happiness."

"You go ahead, let us see how he reacts.”

The next day she took a leave to receive her father. I was waiting for Payal’s message anxiously. Around 10 at night, I received a call and Payal was cracking with joy.

She said, "He wants to meet you."

"What was his reaction?"

"Like every father, he explained the complications that I

am going to face. But he assured me that he will not oppose my decision."

She continued, "He would like to meet you. I have planned a meeting for tomorrow evening in a restaurant."

I reached late. Payal and her father were waiting for me. I shook hands with him and introduced myself.

I said, "Sorry for making you wait."

He responded, "No problem, we did not wait so long."

We sat at our reserved table. I was overly conscious of my actions as he was observing me. He asked me about my parents, siblings and my native place. The waiter came to take the order and I took a sigh of relief because the topic had finally switched to food.

I ordered *masala dosa*, and they both ordered *dahi wada*.

He said, "Payal has told me that you both like each other. I want to know what you have planned. Will your family agree to this marriage?"

Payal interrupted our conversation and said, "Papa, I have already told you that Iqbal's family is a little conservative."

I tried to answer the best possible way but could not understand how to start. I said, "Uncle, we have a genuine feeling for each other..."

The waiter returned with our order. I was aware that I had not actually answered his question. I took a deep breath and said, "I am…I am not sure how my family will react."

I wanted to explain more, but he interjected me and said, "You should not take any decision against your parent's wish."

Payal was perplexed and said, "Papa, you promised me that you would support me and now you are talking like this. I am really confused right now."

"I promised you my support and I will do that. I do want

you to both get married and stay happy but not against Iqbal's parents wishes. At your age, you cannot understand the despair of parents."

If we think from parent's perspective, her father was correct. During old age, the happiness of parents is only with their children. They have sacrificed so much for us. What have we even returned to them?

We obviously can never repay them but we can at least try not to be a reason for their unhappiness. I decided not to go against Payal's or my parent's wishes. If we should ever marry, it must only be with the blessing of our parents. We cannot change the society. I know that it is hard to separate after investing so much of emotions but I believed that there is something good in everything. If we go against our parents' wishes, they will never be able to sleep peacefully. I was lost in my thoughts.

Payal went to the washroom and just then, her father pulled me out of my thoughts and said, "Payal is my only daughter and I try to fulfill all her wishes. I know that she will not be able to handle losing you. You should try to convince your parents and then talk to the relatives who can mediate between you and your parents."

I did not know what to say. It gets very tough to handle the situation when the elders get emotional.

I said, "You can consider me as your son and we both will reach a decision together."

He removed his glasses, placed his right hand over my shoulder, and then said, "Payal has talked so much about you, and no doubt, you are a gentleman."

I hired a taxi for them both. Payal's father and I shook hands and then after bidding goodbye, they left.

It was Monday again, I met Payal at the office, she looked pleasant, and I asked, "Papa, still in town?"

"No, he returned home this morning."

"What did he say about me?" I was curious.

“He liked you and said that you seem to be an honest guy.”

Then, she smiled.

I was flattered by the compliment.

"So, we got the green signal from your father, but not sure how your mom will react to this."

"My mom will not go against my father’s decision on this matter.”

I admired both. Some people live their life without compulsion, without expecting anything from others. Why is it not attainable from everyone? We need a broad mind for this which can discover true happiness inside us.

“There is a positive feeling within me that tells me we will end up together.”

I said, “Do not expect so much. If we are not together then it will be extremely painful for both of us. Let us try and hope for the best.”

I looked at her and asked her, “If things don’t favor us, then you would be really hurt, right?”

She nodded her head expressing no but also wiped the tears rolling down her cheeks. Girls get emotional at the drop of a hat. I said, “Nothing has happened, relax for now.”

I said, "If you cry in the office then others might think that I made you cry.”

We continued with our work.

The advantage of romancing a working woman is the gifts. Every other day she showered me with new clothes, accessories, books, and DVDs.

One day I said, “I am not in a habit of collecting so many clothes. Since college days I have kept only four pairs of shirts and pants at a time."

She said, "You need to change your lifestyle. People judge you by the clothes you wear and the first impression is definitely important"

"I agree with you. It is important to wear decent and clean clothes but it is not necessary to have so many pairs of clothes. When God gives us money then we should not lift our standard of living but our standard of giving," I said in a philosophical manner.

She did not like my words and said, "What do you mean, do you want me to give away my entire salary in charity."

"No, I am not asking you to do the charity. See, If you plan to buy a cloth material from a shopping mall, then you will need to pay a lot more for the brand whereas if you buy the same thing from a non-branded store then you save the extra cost that you have to pay for the brand. So, it is wise to invest that amount of money in the things that we can use for a longer duration like a mobile phone maybe."

She vaguely responded, "I don't know. I feel good when I buy something for you."

The next day was a happy one for me. I received an email saying that I was finally a permanent employee of the company. The curse of the past work experience had finally lifted.

I told Payal and she was elated to hear that.

"I knew that it would happen very soon," she said.

"Boss said that my performance is good. He assured me the permanent payroll immediately. I did not expect all of it to happen so soon."

"We need to celebrate this. Shall we go to the food court?"

We ordered burgers and Coke from McDonalds. We were enjoying and then she popped a question that left me embarrassed.

“You said that you had a scuffle with a girl in your last firm, and that is the reason you lost your job. You did not give me the details. Do you mind sharing it with me?” she asked.

I laughed out loud and said, “I was madly in love with that girl and started acting crazy. I could not forget her even after she said that she did not like me. We once had a conversation and what I said offended her. She then escalated the matter to the higher authority. The result being I lost my job there.”

“I can't believe that you hurt a girl."

Then she asked the name of the girl, and I said, "Her name is Rubina."

“She was so unlucky that she could not understand you," she said after a moment.

I sat down, rested my head, and started stretching my legs. In that moment, I realized that I was completely over from Rubina. I talked about the matter so casually that it was hard for me to believe that I was madly in love with her.

Life is strange. At one point, we feel like that we can’t live without someone and that we will die without him or her. However, time is the most powerful tool that heals any hurt in our heart. Both the girls taught me so much about life. It was because of Rubina’s rejection, I learned to be strong and Payal showed me the meaning of love.

“I am leaving for home this weekend,” I said.

"Is there anything special?" Payal asked.

“I haven’t visited home even once in last few months.”

"Shall I accompany you? Will you introduce me to your parents?" Payal asked with her innocent eyes looking into mine.

"Do you want to meet them?"

“Of course, Yes," she said.

I explained her entire plan. “My parents will not like that we travel together. You can come after a couple of days and say that you are in town to attend a friend’s wedding.”

“That is a good plan, and I will book the ticket."

"I will take care of your ticket and the stay."

We went back to work.

The next morning, I was home.

I headed towards the dining table. Mom served *idly* and *sambhar*. I was eating the same food in Bangalore each day but this tasted so authentic and was full of my Mom’s love. Everyone in the family was so happy to meet me. It was because I was away from home for so long.

“Shall I get the same treatment when I introduce Payal?” I asked myself

“Now Iqbal has a nice job, I think we should start looking for a girl for him,” mom said.

Fouziya added to it and said, "What if he likes someone already?"

“Don’t worry. Bangalore girls aren’t that stupid,” Asif said and chuckled.

I kept quiet as my father was also in the room.

Mom said, “So many people ask me whether Iqbal is ready for marriage."

Asif did not like it and said, "Do not believe all this. Mom is trying to make you feel good. You are not Ranbir Kapoor to get so many marriage proposals."

Dad finished his *idly* first and left for work. I looked at Asif and angrily asked, “How old are you?”

“I am 21 sir." He chuckled again.

"You are not fit to discuss marriage proposals. We will

inform you when you are eligible."

"I am the representative of the new generation. I have equal rights to express my opinion," he said.

The next day, I called Payal. She seemed to be in a hurry, "Shall I come to your house today?"

I said, "Let me check the time when everyone would be home."

I hung up and then casually tried to pull out details from mom. I asked, "What is Papa's plan for today? Will he be home for the evening tea?"

"Yes, I think so. Why? What happened?"

"My colleague is in town for her friend's wedding. We both are working together on the same project. She wants to come and meet you all." She looked at me intently with a confused look and asked suspiciously, "What is your colleague's name Ikku?"

"Her name is Payal." She was bewildered after hearing the name.

"Why does she want to meet us?" She was still confused.

"She will be free by this afternoon, but she has already booked the ticket for tomorrow evening."

My Mom was not convinced and she asked, "She came alone all the way from Bangalore?"

I was not sure why she asked that question.

"She was born and brought up in the city. She has no difficulties in travelling alone."

She rushed to Papa and told him everything. I was looking at them when she spoke. Papa listened patiently and did not react with any questions.

Therefore, finally, it was a green signal. Payal arrived and I guided her over the call. She reached home after 12 noon.

Everyone was already busy discussing something when Payal arrived.

I opened the door and said, "Welcome to my home."

I introduced Payal to my parents.

Papa requested her to take a seat and she settled down on the sofa. I noticed that she was very casual and comfortable. Papa asked, "Where do you stay?"

Payal said, "I am staying in a hotel."

He replied, "Why did you book the hotel? You could have stayed here."

"Hotel is very close to my friend's place, and I found that convenient."

I was curious to know that what was going on in my Mom's mind. She obviously wanted to know the details like whether we met regularly or what kind of relationship we both shared. She was quick to ask.

"Are you both working in the same department?"

I replied, "Yes, we both work at the same place."

She did not like the answer and could not resist asking further questions, "How many members are there in the department?"

Asif could not stop laughing, and that spread to Fouziya and then to me.

I said, "Mom, there are 40 people working on the project, and it is a big team."

Mom must have been relieved. She wanted to ask some more questions but, refrained fearing humiliation.

Mom went into the kitchen. The conversation turned towards Asif and Fouziya. She asked about their studies and career plans. In the meantime, Mom prepared the tea and served it on the table.

She invited everyone but Papa said, “You people carry on, I already had tea.”

Asif looked cunningly at me and asked, “You guys are just friends?"

I stared at him and asked, "What do you mean?"

Asif stammered and asked, "I mean to ask that is Payal your girlfriend?"

I replied, “What did you say yesterday? I remember you saying that Bangalore girls are not fools."

He looked down and muttered, "Sometimes idiots win a lottery.”

We spent some more time chit chatting. Payal looked outside the window.

She said, "It is getting late, and I would like to leave."

I dropped her near the bus stop and returned.

While coming back, I overheard Asif talking to Fouziya, "I think something’s fishy. Ikku comes one day before and his friend comes home the next day, they came with a master plan.”

Fouziya did not encourage him and said, “Your mind is full of rotten thoughts. You find a problem with everything."

Mom was busy cleaning dishes and I went up to her and asked, “What do you think of Payal?”

“I did not notice her that much. She is just your colleague. Am I right?” Mom gave a cold and uninterested reaction.

I lowered my pitch and chose a neutral stance. "She is not just a colleague and we both are in a relationship."

She looked at me to make sure that I was not playing a prank on her. After staring at my face for a couple of seconds her worst fears were confirmed. She realized that I was not lying. For a moment, she seemed completely lost and then after some seconds threw the dishes she was washing. She began shouting at me. “Oh Allah, what is he saying!”

She acted as if the sky had fallen on her.

She held me by my shirt collar and said, "Do you know what you are saying? Did I send you to college and job for this? Nobody in our family has brought shame to the community."

My father and siblings entered the kitchen. Mom started with the same drama that I had seen so many times on TV. She began shouting again. “Did you listen what he said? Ikku has gone crazy! Oh, my lord! That girl has changed him completely. How will I show my face in the community?”

Papa could not understand her howling and asked, "Tell me exactly what he said!”

I interrupted, “I told Mom that, Payal and I are in a relationship.”

Papa tried to handle the situation and said, “Why do you make a scene of everything? He just said they both love each other. What is wrong in that? He knows us well and he will not do anything that shall bring disgrace to our family.”

Papa came close to my face, stared into my eyes and said, “Listen Iqbal! I do not want to give you lectures. You are not a child anymore. You will forget everything and will not keep any contact with that girl.”

I had anticipated the reaction. I took a long deep breath and decided that it was not the time to please them with saying what they wanted to hear. I bluntly said, “Papa, we both love each other a lot and I want to marry her”

My statement shocked my parents. They stood in complete silence but their expressions spoke disapproval, disappointment, and disgust. All of a sudden, I felt something on my face. My father had slapped me hard. I had not anticipated such a violent attack from him.

“Do you even have any idea what you are saying?” We are obviously fools to educate you.

Mom added, "I knew this right away when he introduced that girl."

She resumed her drama and began beating her chest. She then began walking fast like a mad person. Her hair disheveled and the screaming that continued for some more time.

“You both are overreacting! I haven’t committed a crime. I haven’t married her without informing you. We both love each other and I want to marry her.”

“Have you even thought about your sister? Will she get a good proposal after this? I cannot accept this.”

She continued, "Mark my words... if you do anything against our wishes then I will take my life."

I was expecting all of it. When my mom thought that I would not surrender, she threatened me with emotional blackmail. I knew she could never do anything like that. Suicide is a major sin according to Islam and she is a staunch follower of the religion. My only worry was their status in the society. I did not want to be the reason for their humiliation.

I walked out of the house to escape the drama. While I was leaving, I overheard Fouziya and Asif. Asif said, “When I said something is cooking between Ikku and that girl then you did not believe me. See what has happened now.”

Fouziya was not interested in listening and said, "Shut-up."

Although my parents reacted madly, yet I felt light, as I had said what I wanted to say. I was prepared for all this. There was no way I could think to convince them. After witnessing their outburst, I realized that the chances of Payal and I getting married were almost negligible.

Payal called me a couple of times but I did not receive. She called me once more and I answered this time. I said, “Sorry. I am not in a position to talk right now. I will talk to you later.”

"What happened? Is something wrong? Are you Okay?"

I said, "I told them about our relationship and they are against our marriage. I will explain everything in detail when I come to Bangalore.”

She said, "You do not worry and take care of yourself."

I switched off my phone. I was not sure about my future. I decided to give a final answer to Payal. I could not keep her hanging with hope.

I was still emotionally unstable and was not in a condition to decide anything. As wise men say, we should never make promises when we are happy and should never make a decision when we are sad.

I felt calm for some time. Disconnecting from the outer world gave me peace. Mobile phone, computers, Internet, and TV were all invented to give us a better life but I always felt good when I was with nature, places like a hill station.

When I returned home, Asif was trying to fish in troubled waters.

He said to mom, “It is dangerous to send him back to Bangalore.”

Mom said, “You do not say anything. You both are equally dangerous.”

Asif murmured, “Thank you. That is the best compliment that I ever got from you.”

Mom continued further, “You both are paying well for the pain that I had to bear to keep you inside my womb for nine months.”

Mom’s words annoyed Asif and he said, “Why should I

listen for his mistakes? I already have enough on my plate."

I said to my sister, "I am going back to Bangalore tonight."

"You were supposed to stay for some more days," said Fouziya.

"My boss called me up and told me that we have some urgent issues in the project to address. Can you please call the agent to book the ticket?"

She completed the booking when I was busy showering. I had to get rid of the negativity of the day.

Mom insisted on having food and I ate even when I didn't feel like doing so. I knew that it would hurt her if I did not eat. I talked formally to my parents and left for Bangalore. I knew that they would miss me and were worried for me.

Chapter 11

As soon as I reached Bangalore, I went to the office. On my way, I received a call from Payal and asked her to join me in the office canteen. Payal was anxious.

"Are you OK?"

I did not answer.

"How was your journey? When did you reach?" I inquired.

"I reached early morning. So, tell me about your parents' reaction…"

I took a bite of a sandwich and then said, "As expected my mom created a huge drama and threatened that she will kill herself if I marry you."

"What about your father?"

"Papa's behavior also changed when I explained that we both plan to get married."

Payal listened with an expressionless face. She took a pause and then tried to solace me with her words.

"We did all we could. At least we won't regret that we did not even try."

She was again lost in her own thoughts and then said, "I was happy to meet your family. I know that they do not have anything against me. We are just unlucky."

It was this one quality in Payal that I admired the most. She had no regrets in life. "I am unlucky because I am going to lose you."

Payal gazed at me and said, "If I convert to your faith, will things be okay?"

"I do not want you to change your religion for this reason. I can never allow you to do this. It would be injustice not only to you but me as well. It is against my principles."

I became emotionally unstable. My new motto in life was to find a suitable match for Payal. I knew that if Payal did not take a practical decision, then she would definitely ruin her life. I could never let that happen.

I am a firm believer of the saying that there is a time for everything. Payal was crazy in love and therefore her mind was not allowing her to think of anything. It is when she would get older, her priorities and views towards life would change.

Payal was a girl who never planned anything in life. It was my duty to guide her. We should experience all the phases of life fully. We never get a chance to relive past or make corrections. I broke the silence and said, "You need to seriously start thinking about other proposals."

"You know that I am not mentally prepared to marry any other guy." I was shocked at her reply.

I continued with my mission and asked, "How can you presume that you are not prepared when you haven't even given it a try?"

I took a deep breath and then continued, "Listen, I understand your emotions and your state of mind but all of this is just transient. When you get married and have children, your life will be different. Your husband and your kids will become your world and nothing else would matter."

Payal was still not persuaded. I did not know what else

to do.

"Do you know something…After some years you will not even remember me."

She did not like my words and angrily said, "Shut up!"

"Are you trying to get rid of me so that you can live a happy family life? Don't worry! I will not cross your path in any phase of life."

Our conversation took a different turn. I needed to explain myself. "How can you even think something like that? I just want you to be happy and live a happy life. It is the only reason. I suggest that we part ways."

Payal felt guilty for her words. She quickly said, "I am so sorry."

In the meantime, she had already used half of the tissue papers in wiping away her tears.

"Do you think it is so easy to forget everything? I don't think that there is anything wrong in keeping in touch. We can be good friends even after I get married to someone else."

"We both understand that what we have for each other is pure but some other person might not."

I had already helped her to think logically about the matter. I continued. "Let us not complicate things. I feel it is better if we don't keep any contact."

I took a pause for some time and said, "Let us think about it later, for now, I am happy that you changed your mind regarding marriage."

"No, I haven't changed my mind. I will accept any proposal only after your marriage."

I couldn't stop myself from laughing. "You are so stubborn. It is impossible to convince you."

I relaxed in the chair a bit and started thinking of things

to say that would convince her.

"You will not agree but the truth is that in our society, it is not difficult for a man, even in his 40s to get a good marriage proposal. It is not the same for women. Also, if a man wants then he can live life alone but the society makes it very difficult for a woman to do that."

I knew that it was a debatable topic but I said it to convince Payal.

"What is the point in getting married when my happiness does not matter? I may not become a good wife and might ruin other person's life as well."

I knew that those were the words of endearment towards me, "Do you remember the days when we were just colleagues? You did not even talk to me. Did you know that you will get so close to me? See, how everything changed. We started liking each other as deeply as we come to know each other personally. It is basic human nature."

She looked at me and said, "I feel like you are going to forget me and will move on quickly with life. I know that it is for the best, but thinking of it scares me."

I held her hand firmly and said, "Do you think it is possible to forget you that easily? You are the true treasure of my life and only person in my life who has loved me without any expectations. You were the one who came into my life when I was at my lowest. I believe God sent you as an angel to be by my side, otherwise, I would have gone insane."

There were tears in her eyes, I was distracted by them and it hurt me that she was so broken.

"It is not that I don't have any feelings, but I have to be strong. We both are mature and need to be practical. Some things are beyond our control. We need to decide now as it impacts others too. I don't want us to be the reason of our parents' suffering," I said.

She kept looking down and stayed quiet. I knew that even she agreed to what I had said.

"You are talking to your parents today and asking them to start looking for proposals for you."

She nodded in silence and I was finally relieved that she agreed. We sat together for a while and then went back to our work desks.

After a couple of days, Payal began feeling ignored. She once said that she found my behavior strange.

I replied, "Why did you say that?"

"You are ignoring me at work, and you don't even talk on the phone every night like before. And even if you talk, you are quick to disconnect the call," she said.

"Do you know how difficult it is for me if you change suddenly? I feel the night would never end. I stop myself from calling you back so that I do not disturb your sleep." She was heartbroken but what Payal didn't know was that I never slept peacefully since we broke up.

"Look Payal, we need to stop talking late at night. This is going to happen someday. It is best if we distance ourselves sooner."

"Iqbal, life is not a software project where you have the high-level design and write the code according to the design. In real life, we don't even know if we will be alive tomorrow or not," she said.

She took a deep breath and said, "We decided to break off our relationship and we are also open to other marriage proposals but let us not plan too much. Let us please be happy until the time we are together."

I kept quiet and then she said, "I am going to book tickets for a movie this evening."

The movie finished at 11 pm. I was riding back home to

drop Payal on my bike.

“Have you talked to your parents about our decision?” I asked.

"Yes, I explained everything that happened at your home."

“They must be happy to know that you came back safely.” She did not answer back.

We were riding in silence when I saw a group of motorcycles behind us. They were cheering very loudly and were emitting weird sounds. I counted, I could see four in the side mirror. I assumed that they were returning from a party. I slowed down to let them pass but they did not want to overtake and that’s when I realized that they were following us.

I was scared. I had no idea what to do. I was even more horrified as Payal was with me. She held my shoulder with a tight grip and said, “Iqbal I am frightened. What will we do?”

“Quickly call people at the office who stay nearby and tell them our location,” I muttered.

After 5-10 minutes of riding, we, unfortunately, had reached a deserted area. They took the advantage of it and encircled us.

They snatched the phone from Payal’s hands. I knew that it was a planned trap.

I got down from the bike and Payal stood next to me closely, holding my hand firmly. The biker began making jokes and imitating. I did not find anything funny in that, I was scared.

One of the bikers nudged me and asked, “Oh, so you are the hero. For which Jihadi Group are you working?” It took me a few moments to realize that those guys were sent by Payal’s ex-boyfriend, Vishal. Vishal had threatened Payal a lot but when he failed in his attempts to separate us, he approached the extremist group in the city to take revenge on us. My only relief was that they wouldn't do anything to Payal. I had read in the newspaper a few days back that the Hindu extremists believed that a conspiracy regarding an International Terrorist was being organized, where the Muslim boys used romance as a medium to fool Hindu girls and then forcibly convert them to their religion. They named the term as 'Love Jihad'. A number of programs on TV and other media aimed at protecting Hindu girls from such acts.

Payal shouted, "I know that Vishal has sent you. Shame on you and shame on him! This is my personal matter and it is a shame that you drag religion into this."

One of the bikers answered her back, "It is our duty to protect our faith and values. These people have ruined our culture and have robbed our assets. They do not respect our motherland and mock our God and beliefs. We can't let that happen and will tell them that we are here to protect our people."

Payal was quick to reply, "I just saw your antics, and how you respect your motherland! By the way, who gave you the authority to protect 'our' people? You yourself are involved in violence. You beat up men and women mercilessly. Which Veda has allowed violence towards women?"

I did not have any idea that what would happen next but I tried to calm down the situation. I said, "Guys! There is no point in fighting. We both already understood the complexities and have decided to not get married. In fact, our parents are looking for suitable matches for us."

I tried to explain my logic but as expected they mocked at me and said, "Oh! So, this is the 'use and throw approach'. Why can't you find a girl from your own community to use and then dump her?"

I was infuriated but I understood the results of my burst

out. I decided to calm down and in a controlled tone I said, “Mind your language.”

It did not go well with him. He came really close to me and said, “What will you do if I do not mind my language?”

“I am not obliged to give you people an explanation but I still did. Give me some respect and leave us alone,” I said.

He walked towards me and asked, “Hey…Do you want respect?”

I stepped back but he slapped me hard a couple of times and said, “Here! Take your respect!”

Payal tried to stop him but I asked her to move back as I did not want things to go out of hand.”

He stood extremely close and in a loud pitch, said, “Hey! If you want to be a hero in front of the girl, then come and smash me!”

They were clearly provoking me but I was not a fool to get into a fight. They were four in number and would have beaten me up if I would have responded to their provocation. Payal reminded me the same thing and said, “Iqbal, do not say a word to them.”

They tried everything, from abusing to making faces to brushing against my body but I did not utter a single word and kept looking down.

They finally said, "Are you even a man?"

Payal responded quickly, "Four people attacking an individual is not heroism."

They looked at me and mocked, "Fooling the girls of our religion in the name of love and then converting them to Islam is Heroism. Am I right?"

Anger was building up inside me and I finally wanted to fight but they spared us with a warning.

Their leader warned us. “This is my first and final warning

to you. We will not leave you like this. Our people will keep an eye on you. We will not show any mercy if we catch you both together in the future. Don't act smart to approach the police else the consequences will be worst. I hope you will follow my words," he said.

Payal took a sigh of relief and then wiped away sweat drops from my forehead. I felt so drained. I feebly kicked my bike and asked Payal to sit. We were about to leave and just then one of the guys in the group said, "This is the last time you both are riding a bike together."

I accelerated and came out of the area. I looked into the mirror a few times but could not find anyone following us.

After that unfateful experience, I was relieved that we escaped a possible fight. It was late in the evening and we finally reached Payal's house. Before leaving, she asked, "Do you want to approach the police?"

"No, Let us end the matter here. I don't think they respect any religion. We people have so many Hindu friends who are supporting and genuinely help us. I know Hindu religion better than those goons. Vishal is a sick man to do this. I did not take your words seriously when you first told me about this. Let us talk about it tomorrow. Do not worry about anything."

I zoomed away and reached home. I tried to sleep but all in vain. I spent the night tossing and turning as my mind was extremely disturbed. The incident had left a deep impact on my subconscious. The body odour and the smell of *paan* that their leader was chewing, refused to leave my senses.

A couple of weeks passed. We tried to maintain a distance. One day while talking to Payal over coffee, I said, "I am going to resign."

She gasped in disbelief. For a moment, she thought that I was joking.

"Yes, it is true. I sent the resignation email last week. Boss tried to convince me to stay with a promise of pay hike but I have made up my mind. I have asked him today to allow the relieving process. So, basically, this is my last week in office."

She still could not believe that I had not told her about such a big decision. I purposefully kept her out of it because I knew that she wouldn't let me leave.

She said, "I am so shocked that you have done this without informing me."

"Payal, this is the best decision. Do not worry about my career and I already have good offers from a couple of companies." I began my explanation in a convincing way.

She said, "I don't believe that you have any other offers. It looks like you are playing with your career."

"I swear in the name of God that I have other options. I have been jobless once, I know the difficulties when you have responsibilities on your shoulders. I will not do anything foolish."

I made the decision mainly for three reasons. The first and foremost reason was that it was easier for both, Payal and me to forget and come out of the relationship. I wanted Payal to start a new relationship with an open mind. I knew that she was not ready, and my presence would create more trouble.

The second reason was, I did not want anything bad to happen. The incident that happened a few days back had shaken me. For me, it was important that Payal stays away from any problem. Also, I did not want to be the reason for her embarrassment and worry.

The third reason was that I did not want us to be the cause for our parents' worry. They were aware of our relationship and I did not want any trepidation because of us. Most importantly, I knew that my mother would be relieved.

I could not think of a way to convince Payal. She thought that all my reasons were irrelevant and that I was thinking too much.

"Are you scared of the threats from those rowdies?" Payal asked.

I was expecting this question from her and then explained, "I am not scared. If we were to get married, then I would have faced any threat in the world to be with you. But you need to understand that if anything goes wrong then you are the one who will have to face more troubles. I think it is better to be on the safer side."

Payal was still not convinced, "Why do you want to be on the safer side always? If we get scared of everything, then we cannot live our life. As you said, we can go to the police station."

I answered her. "I thought about this. Do you think it is easy for common citizens like us to get police protection?

I think it is better to avoid it. There will be many useless questions and lot of drama. My main reason for leaving the company is not to escape from those people but to escape your mind. I know that you will not marry anyone else if I am around you. I truly pray that you get the strength to bear all this. You have always respected my decisions, and this is my final request to you."

"Won't you miss me?" she asked with tears of pain.

Obviously yes, but I did not want to say that to hurt her more.

I said, "I am not saying to be practical, but what I want to say is that your life has just begun. Life will throw many challenges at you. You should not give up and face them strongly."

I was resorting to philosophy to avoid her questions. I know that it is easier said than done.

She was now full of tears and asked again, “Won’t you miss me?”

I tried to answer this time, "Yes, I am going to miss you. But what I was trying to say is that it is all part and parcel of our life."

Not sure whether my answer was rude, but I wanted to convey that she has an amazing life waiting for her.

She said, "I don't know about you but I will miss you a lot. I have no idea how I will handle your absence.”

I wanted to make her feel better. “I have been through the same phase when I was madly in love with Rubina. I thought I wouldn’t be able to live without her. I tried to overcome and move on but everything failed. It was you who helped me to come out of her thoughts and that madness that I felt. I want you to do the same. After some years, you won’t even remember my name.”

As soon as I finished speaking, she started sobbing.

“Please stop crying and let us get back to work. It is getting late.”

We resumed working and I noticed that Payal looked muddled. I hushed, “Promise me that you will not cry anymore in life.” She nodded and I was relieved.

It was my last day in office. I completed all the formalities and received the relieving letter. My colleagues arranged a small farewell for me in the evening. People spoke some words about me, about work and personal terms. It was good to hear such words but my smile hid the pain of desertion. In the end, I shook hands with everyone.

One of the colleagues asked me, "What is the plan for future?"

"I have a couple of offers and yet to make the decision."

When I shook hands with Payal, she said that she would

accompany me to the office gate.

It was much more difficult for me to leave Payal than I had anticipated. We sat in the corridor and I tried my best to say goodbye on a happy note.

I said, "You can call me whenever you need me, and I will be there for you. Take care of yourself and be happy always. I am unlucky that I cannot have you in my life. I never got what I needed the most. Take care of your parents as you are the only one they have. It is the kindness of God that you have such loving and supporting parents. You are the best person I have ever known in my life. I am sure that God has some better plans for you."

She started crying and I did not say anything else. I wanted to see her happy face as my last memory of her.

She said, "I know that we will now be out of touch. Please inform me when something important happens in your life. Like your engagement, marriage, babies…"

Her emotions choked her and she stopped speaking.

I kept looking at her and in that moment, I lost control and broke into tears. She hugged me and said, "I am sorry for making you cry."

I quickly recovered and said, "I want you to say goodbye with a happy face."

With a heavy heart, I left.

The loss of a loved one is one of the most tragic and devastating things a person can endure.

That was the first time in my life I cried so badly.

Chapter 12

Six months passed.

My dear Payal, I wish I could have more time with you so that I could tell you that I had one of my best smiles with you. I wrote in my diary.

My new office and a new environment could not help much to overcome Payal's thoughts.

It was a difficult phase in my life. I tried to compare my separation from Payal with the earlier phase I lived with Rubina. The comparison is an integral part of our life.

There was a huge difference between the two. I was angry and frustrated when Rubina walked out of my life. I wanted to forget and erase all my memories of her and then start a new life. But my break up with Payal had me running from the beautiful reminiscences that she gifted. Which one was more painful? Both!

I did not stop my father from looking for marriage proposals.

Papa said, "I will send the photographs and profiles to your email. I will call the girl's parents if you like any one of them."

I hung up and checked my emails. I downloaded all the photographs. There were total 6 pictures and I shortlisted three.

I checked the profiles of all three that I had selected. One of them was taller than me, so I began looking closely into the other two. Then, I compared qualifications of the two. One was intermediate pass and the other one was Bachelor in Arts. I decided to go with the second one. I read her name in the profile. It was a sweet name, Naziya.

I told Papa that I liked one of the six profiles he had sent me. As expected he was glad and enthusiastic.

After a couple of hours, he called me again and this time he had the full history of the girl's family. From our conversation, I could sense that he wanted to analyze the dowry to be demanded.

He said, "The girl's father has gifted three hundred sovereigns of gold during her elder sister's wedding."

Don't get surprised. This is very common in Kerala.

After an hour Papa called me again. "He is a building contractor. I heard that he has so much of black money. He must have invested in real estate," he said.

He kept calling me every other hour until late night. I could get some sleep only after turning my phone to silent mode.

There were so many missed calls from Papa when I checked my phone in the morning. I called him back and mom picked up the call.

"Your father is busy making arrangements. He is so happy that you accepted the proposal."

"Who said that I accepted the proposal?" It was a bit shocking to me.

"What are you saying? Your father has gone to the *Qazi* for an auspicious wedding date."

"How can you conclude that my marriage is fixed even

before I meet the girl? How do you know about the girl's choice? First, arrange a meeting with the girl."

My tickets were booked for home as Papa was quick to organize a meeting that weekend.

Fouziya was there in the yard when I reached home, she said, "I liked the girl in the photo."

It is difficult to talk when family members are around. I wanted to avoid the traditional ceremony of *roka* and decided to meet her at a private place.

"I don't want to visit the girl's house. I just want to meet her alone somewhere out like a coffee shop. I only want Fouziya to accompany me."

My intention was to meet her in a comfortable environment where we both could talk openly.

But my parents thought that it was against the traditions and un-Islamic.

"I heard that they are an orthodox family and are against following western culture. I am not sure if they will agree," Papa said.

I failed to understand that how was it against the culture and religion to talk to the girl before making an important decision like marriage.

Papa made multiple calls to many people. I realized that my demand of meeting the girl was being misunderstood. I received a call from my maternal uncle, "I heard that you want to conduct an interview before selecting the girl? They are against it Ikku," he said.

I knew that it was a waste talking to my family so I decided to talk to the girl's father instead. I called him up and after initial greeting, I explained my intentions politely. To my surprise, he understood and assured me a meeting and even suggested a few places.

"I think Bekal fort is a good place to meet," I said.

The venue and date were fixed but I was scared. When we decide to buy a phone, we read so many reviews on different websites, but I had to make the most important decision of my life with just one meeting. I felt helpless.

Bekal fort is one of the main attractions of northern Kerala and a favorite tourist spot. The fort aligned with the Arabian Sea is what makes it so beautiful. During monsoons, it is a breathtaking view as it is surrounded by greenery.

So many movies have explored presenting the beauty of the fort on the silver screen but I feel director Maniratnam did the best work in his movie, 'Bombay'. The steps across the area are well-maintained and add beauty to it. The sea breeze is a delight. I remember how the actor is lost in the beauty of the fort in the song, 'Tu Hi Re'. My phone rang and I remembered that the purpose of my visit was something else.

"Am I speaking to Iqbal?"

It was a sweet voice from the other side and I assumed that she was the girl that I was going to meet. I gave her the directions.

After a couple of minutes, I noticed two women walking towards me. One of them was dressed in a *burqa*. I assumed her to be the girl's elder sister.

"She is my younger sister, Naziya." The lady in the *burqa* spoke.

Then, we all introduced ourselves.

Naziya was almost similar to my imagination. She had a slim body structure and a small cute face. Her complexion was wheatish, she was dressed in a blue *salwar* suit and had a black shawl over it. Her shade of dress matched mine completely. I was dressed in a blue shirt and black jeans. I liked the coincidence.

I introduced them to my sister. Naziya greeted with a smile.

Naziya's smile resembled that of Payal's.

I stared at her. I realized that she actually looked a lot like Payal. I subconsciously chose the girl who looked like Payal.

Our subconscious mind is the biggest mystery, and it can do things without us knowing.

I wanted to talk to Naziya in private but did not know how to ask.

In the meantime, Naziya's sister walked up to Fouziya and said, "Let them talk separately for some time."

We were both walking on the shore. It felt weird as we both were strangers who had met for a purpose of marrying each other. We had no idea about each other's lives like character, likes, habits, goals and interests. It is how our Indian arranged-marriage system works and surprisingly it is successful to an extent.

I was blank and couldn't think of anything to start a conversation. I tried thinking and finally asked, "Naziya from where have you completed your education?"

She answered promptly, "I studied at St. Angels College in Mangalore. I was the day scholar and I am someone who cannot live in hostels. Have you traveled any time in local trains? It is a fantastic experience to travel in the ladies compartment and then listen to the strangers gossiping. I enjoyed traveling for five years."

My first impression about this girl was that she talks non-stop but I liked that. After a few years of marriage, the beauty begins to fade away but the character, smartness and knowledge are what we should look for in a partner.

But how could I know everything about her in a single meeting? I could not judge her knowledge by asking who the Finance Minister of our country is. It was important for me that girl I marry should not be dumb. Was I thinking too much?

I asked about her hobbies and interests. She spoke till I changed the topic. She had a lot to say about everything.

I asked about her family and she told me about everyone including her distant cousins and other relatives. The list was endless and I soon began to regret asking. It was surprising to me that how she was able to talk so casually to someone whom she had met for the first time.

Then I asked, "What are your career plans?" All of a sudden, she fell silent as if I had asked her something that she had never thought about in her life.

She looked down and said, "My father said that husband is the one who is going to decide that after the marriage."

It amused me. "You are the one who should decide about your career and marriage, not someone else," I said.

I could read hesitation in her eyes.

"Do you have anything to ask?"

I encouraged her, "You can ask anything you want..."

She asked, "Do you want to take your wife to Bangalore after marriage?"

I laughed and cross-questioned her, "Do you have a problem with leaving your parents and settling in another city?" She nodded in acceptance.

I said, "We can think about it later. Do not worry about it."

Naziya is affable, and I liked this particular character trait. I do not talk much until I get very fond of someone. It is true that the opposites attract and I started liking her. I restrained myself from asking further questions because I did not have the patience to listen anymore.

Then I said, "Let us leave now. It is getting late." We left for the day.

On our way back home, Fouziya asked, "What was there to talk for so long?"

I did not answer.

As expected, she asked the next question, "Did you like the girl?"

I did not respond to that question as well.

After a couple of moments, I asked her, "What about you? Did you like her?"

Fouziya said, "Yes, I liked her very much. She is really cute."

I was bewildered. I liked Naziya's open-mindedness, but I was still unable to judge whether it was smartness or dumbness. I thought a lot and finally decided to say yes.

We reached home and I noticed the anxiety on everyone's faces. Fouziya explained everything in detail. In the meantime, I took a shower.

When I returned, Papa asked me, "What is your opinion about the girl?"

Everybody was so anxious to hear my answer. I said, "I can accept this proposal on one condition…we will go ahead with the proposal only if we don't demand dowry. It will be same for all the proposals that you find for me."

Papa's face became pale.

Papa again made multiple calls to many people. He was forced to accept my condition as I had sacrificed my love for their happiness. After a few hours, he said, "We have decided to arrange a small function for your engagement in the coming week."

Within no time, both the families agreed and my marriage was fixed with Naziya. I called my childhood friends, Mustafa and Sajid and informed them about my engagement. They were happy for me and congratulated me for my new chapter in life.

We decided to invite only close relatives and friends for the engagement. I prepared a list and called them personally. Most of them promised to attend the function.

That night when I lay in my bed, I replayed all the major life incidents in my mind. I realized that no matter how much we plan, there is always some powerful force that decides our destiny, maybe it is God. I believe in a supreme power and I feel that if we do not disturb his plans then something good will happen to us.

According to the customs, we had to buy gold ornaments and new dresses for the girl. The next day, I went shopping with my family and bought a gold necklace worth five sovereigns and a maroon colored *salwar*. I also bought clothes for my family. My account balance took a major dip in just one day.

One of my friends said, "This is just the beginning."

The function was planned at her house. It seemed like a grand affair. All of Naziya's relatives were eager to see me. My family shared the same excitement. I was dressed in a blue and white *kurta-pyjama.*

I was the center of attraction and enjoyed the royal treatment. It was a two-story house with wooden interior. I walked to the hall and I saw Naziya sitting, dressed in a green outfit. My mother then gave her the gifts that we had brought.

Islamic tradition prohibits touching of the girl before the marriage. Therefore, I was not allowed to give her the gifts. Everyone wanted to take a picture of me and that was when I felt like a celebrity.

In Indian weddings, elder people are treated with huge

respect. The major decisions about the ceremony are taken by the elder members of the families and the bride and bridegroom do not have a say in it.

The first point of discussion was dowry of course. Since I had my point very clear to my father, he did not demand anything. The next point was the date and venue of the wedding ceremony. *Qazi* looked for auspicious dates and finally according to my Papa's wish, his favorite hall was booked.

I looked towards Naziya, and she bonded well with my family. In the meantime, one of the persons announced the updates.

I was lost in my own thoughts. Did I have any other choice? Did I dream of my wedding happening this way or was I bowing down to my family's happiness? Life is all about compromises.

I had a choice of postponing my marriage for a couple of years, but I followed my inner instinct. We all returned home after greetings.

Everything happened so quickly that I did not even inform Payal about my engagement. I then remembered the last promise that I made to her. I was still not sure about the state of mind she would be in during that time.

I did not want to unnecessarily disturb her when she must have moved on. My engagement would not make any difference to her life.

I talked to Mustafa about my worries. "It is really tough to understand a girl's mind. Even if you both broke up mutually, she might still be living in a hope that you might return someday. I think it is better to let her know. By doing this you will help her move on in life," he said.

I picked my mobile and called Payal's number. She had the same hello-tune from the movie Jab We Met. '*Tum se hi din hota hai, surmaiye shaam aati, tumse hi, tumse hi...har ghadi saans aati hai, zindagi kehlati hai, tumse hi, tumse hi'*

The song brought back all the memories that I had created with her. Nostalgia filled me with all the lovely moments that we had spent together.

Earlier I used to get irritated by the song because I had to listen to it each time I called Payal.

It was that day when I realized what I had lost. The more we get attached to something, the more painful is the loss. I wished there was some magic that would help me get over all my emotions for Payal.

If we lose a valuable, there is still hope and can build an empire again but even after winning the world I would still not be able to recover from the loss.

After a couple of rings, Payal received the call, "Hello Iqbal."

I noticed that she did not call me Ikku.

"Hello, how are you?"

She said, "It is nice to hear your voice."

“I called to inform you about something."

She was silent and I knew that she had guessed what I wanted to convey. "I got engaged, and will marry in six months."

She reacted with pleasure. "Wow, congratulations.”

Then she inquired about the girl, her qualifications, and the background. She requested me to send her photographs. I assured her that I would send through WhatsApp after the call.

I felt that she did not have any regrets. But I was not sure whether she was pretending or had actually moved on with the life.

“Why didn’t you tell me before? I would have attended the engagement. I think you did not want me to be there,” she said.

"I was confused. But it is nice to know that you are happy in your life."

"How can you say that I am happy? I am glad that everything is happening according to your plan."

"What do you mean?”

“My parents bought a marriage proposal last week. We will accept this proposal most probably.”

I felt a lot of different emotions on hearing this. I felt happy for her but at the same time, I was going to be a ‘nobody’ to her. We both were going to commit to other relationships and would not be able to talk or meet each other. I had not realized that I would feel this way when I got engaged but when I spoke to her, I felt a huge wall between us.

She said, "So this is the end of our story then.”

I was speechless and a future without Payal seemed like a difficult reality to accept. She understood that I was weeping within and tried to console me.

“As you always say that a new relationship will help you come out of all the pain. You should look at it positively. If you committed to someone then it is your responsibility to give proper time to the girl.”

She said few more words before hanging up the call. "You are a nice person by heart, and only good things will happen to you. You must invite me to your wedding, and I will surely attend."

My heart was heavy and I began feeling gloomy. I locked myself in my room and completely broke down into tears. I wanted to vent out all the pain and other emotions inside me. For a moment, I thought that religion had created more harm than good to the world. Religion should help to unite people and should teach to love one another unconditionally. Is there any fault in practicing?

Unfortunately, I was the victim of the so-called system.

I felt too distant from Payal but I had wonderful memories to cherish forever. Sometimes, we do not know the value of a moment until it becomes a memory.

Chapter 13

I woke up at 11 in the morning after having seen a weird dream. There was a 'Good morning' message from Naziya in my inbox. I came back to the real world and realized that I was on the verge of a new relationship.

I had another one week of vacation. Holidays are always fun.

I had breakfast and checked out to the courtyard.

I replied to Naziya's text but she did not message me further.

I called her after some time. "Hello Naziya, How are you doing?"

"Why didn't you call me after the function? Is it something that your parents and friends did not like about me?" Naziya asked in a single breath.

"Everyone liked you so much. I was just busy with some work." These are the small things that are extremely important to girls.

"Do you mind going out with me this evening?" I said casually.

She was shocked for a moment as she did not expect this question, "Outside...what do you mean?"

"Perhaps, we can go to a coffee shop...or else...we can go to the beaches and spend time."

"Let me discuss with my sister and call you back."

Naziya called me back after some time.

"I have so many cousins who are elder to me and have already got married. They had never gone outside with their fiancé before the marriage."

I asked, "Is it because meeting the fiancé before the wedding is against Islam? If that is the case then even speaking on the phone before the wedding is against the faith. Do you know that?"

"I do not think it is wrong as all my cousins were speaking on the phone."

I thought it was very childish of her. "Why don't you have your own opinion? You are a grown-up lady, and you should be able to make your own decisions. It is not necessarily right if your cousins and relatives are doing it."

I knew that Naziya was young and had just graduated from college but I expected more maturity from her. She worried about what her parents and relatives think but some people can even handle that without upsetting the other person. She was unable to make her own decisions and depended on her sister's or cousin's guidance. I tried to solace myself thinking that she was still very young.

I noticed her childishness in our first meeting but chose not to judge a book by its cover. She failed to create a good impression about herself. Our subconscious unknowingly picks up information about the people we meet and then creates their image in our minds. When we believe that someone is a nice person then even if the judiciary and the law system punishes them, our mind will not be able to accept it.

I always thought that a wife should be someone we can

trust completely. I decided not to judge her as everyone has good and bad traits and it is okay if the good qualities outnumber the bad ones.

"So what did you decide? Would you like to go out?"

As expected, she did not have a convincing answer. "Let me talk to my mom and will let you know."

"Naziya, I do not understand - what is there to discuss so much? We are going to get married. I would like to meet outside to understand each other better. It is important to know each other's interests, likes, and priorities. I have no other intentions."

She was silent, and I continued, "First you wanted to talk to your sister and then with your mother. So next would be your father, aunties, uncles, friends..."

I paused for a moment and expected a response from her.

I continued, "Listen Naziya, Suppose if you ask more people then you may confuse yourself more. Now decide whether you would like to come out with me or not?"

"I…I can come to Panambur beach this evening."

"That is good. I will be there at 5 pm."

I reached on time but Naziya wasn't there even after I waited for 30 minutes. She was the third woman in my life who was always late. Waiting for people annoyed me a lot. I tried to pass my time by playing mobile games.

Some more time passed and I lost patience. I was scared that she might read anger on my face. I tried to calm down and thought that we all do silly and stupid things when we are angry. We all need to control it and will never be able to have a good relationship with the opposite gender due to it.

Girls appreciate guys who are calm and composed. I decided to make an attempt at being in my senses and stay collected. It was our first date and I wanted to make it a memorable one.

I think everything has an expiration date and it is better to enjoy the present to its fullest or else it would be late when we realize the importance of those moments. I hated Payal before knowing her personally. So I don't feel that first impressions are that important in a relationship. I hoped that it was the case with Naziya too.

Girls take a longer time to understand and judge people. They start liking the other person only after knowing him completely. So I decided to give our relationship some time and see where it goes.

I was pulled out of my thoughts by Naziya's words. "Sorry for making you wait."

We sat on a bench facing the sea. People usually visited to witness the beauty of sunset and sunrise. As wise people say that it is only the sunrise and sunset that are constant, everything else is unpredictable.

The smell of her perfume filled the environment. I did not like it. It smelled like something that she picked up from a stall near the Masjid street. I decided to gift her perfume of a good brand on our next date.

She sat a little away from me and I watched Naziya drinking water from her bottle after every few minutes. She was dressed in a yellow dress and looked pretty.

She was using her phone and it felt like that she was trying to show off her iPhone.

"Is it an iPhone?"

"Yes, iPhone 5s, my uncle bought it from Dubai."

She was satisfied because she successfully communicated that she owned iPhone. I could read that from her face.

"Did you have any trouble in reaching here?"

"Oh my gosh! I came here without letting anyone know. I

am not sure what will happen if my parents come to know."

“Nobody is aware that you are coming here?"

"Only my sister knows," she muttered.

"What is the nature of your job?” Naziya asked.

“I am a Software Engineer, and we develop software."

"What do you mean by developing software?” She was curious.

I tried explaining in a layman language. "Have you seen the computer software or websites?"

She did not have an idea, and I tried to simplify the things.

"Do you use Facebook?"

“Yes, I have an account on Facebook and I am a regular user."

Thank God. She at least knew Facebook.

“We develop and maintain similar kinds of software.”

I was happy that we were finally talking about sensible things but then she said something which made me rethink about her and my decision of marrying her.

What was that question?

The conversation began on a normal note. She looked excited and said, "I like beaches. Whenever I get the chance to visit with friends or relatives, I do not miss."

She still made sense so far. No problem at all. Most of us like to visit the beaches.

Then she said, "What about you? Don't you visit beaches in Bangalore?"

It was a stupid question but I still played along and thought that curiosity is a nice trait.

I said, "There are no beaches in Bangalore.”

"Oh is it? I thought beaches are everywhere”

It felt like a sea wave that pulled and dumped me into a remote area.

It is okay if we are not good at general knowledge or do not have a keen interest in geography as a subject. Even I can't exactly locate Orissa on the map but when someone says that they think all the cities in the world have beaches then it is sheer ignorance. The underlying message was that Naziya's world only comprised of her parents, cousins, aunties, and uncles. She was not interested in anything else in the world.

I thought of testing her general knowledge. I asked, "Do you know who the Indian President is?"

She looked a little perplexed and said, "I am not interested in politics."

It was very difficult for me to control my laughter. She did not know the answer to such an easy thing and answered as if I had asked whether she liked pizza or not.

"Don't you think it is important to know basic things about our country?"

She kept quiet for some time and then said, "I know it is important, but I do not like it."

"What are your likes then?"

"I like movies. I am a big fan of Shahrukh Khan and watch all his movies."

She then talked for approximately 15 minutes explaining what kind of movies she liked and watched. She also told me about people with whom she loved to watch movies. She then began narrating the story of her favorite ones.

I interrupted her. "I have also watched this film."

I had to dumb down myself to effectively communicate with her.

I always thought that I should be able to discuss anything

and everything with my wife. She should be one whose advice and suggestions are valuable to me. She should be able to guide the children for their bright future. My wife should have a mind of her own and should know how to take responsibilities of her actions. When there are misunderstandings then she should be able to suppress them for the good. I know that we never get everything that we want and it is greedy of us to expect so much. Naziya had none of the qualities that I was looking for in my wife. Did her beauty compensate her tantrums?

Absolutely, Naziya is good looking and well-spoken girl.

I said to myself, "Do I need to give more time to her?"

I was confused.

Also, it was 'sin' in our society to meet and understand the person before getting married.

Will it be okay if I change my decision? I was adamant to know and discuss things with the girl against my family's wishes. It also did not go well with many of my relatives. I remember that one of my maternal uncles said, "I met my wife for the first time on my wedding day. What happened to me? By God's grace, I have six healthy children."

It is difficult to make people realize that having healthy children isn't the motto of life. They think that the more you produce kids, the more chances you have of living a secured old age. Arranged marriage is a luck based thing. People still believe that God has planned that who our life partner and no need to worry about it. It was true that I had asked for time to understand the girl better. I was looking for decent education and she had it. My instincts said that she couldn't be a dumb person being a graduate. I spoke to her a couple of times later but was still confused about the decision.

I asked myself, "Do I need to take the risk? Or should I leave everything to luck?"

Naziya asked, "Is anything troubling you?"

I realized that I should not make my annoyance obvious. It was me who had invited her and she agreed to come. Also, technically she had not done anything wrong with me.

I pretended to be happy. Will I be able to pretend all my life?

I had so many doubts. What would be the consequences if we break the relationship? Do I need to hint Naziya that I was not happy with her?

Naziya did not have any idea about what was going in my mind.

"Do you have many friends?"

I said, "Yes, I have many friends, some of them are close to me."

Then I continued, "What about you?"

"Yes, I also have so many friends. I keep in touch with them regularly. We contact through Whatsapp and Facebook. We meet occasionally and plan out some fun thing to do."

Naziya asked, "I hope you will let me keep in touch with my friends after the marriage. Am I right?"

"Why did you ask that? Why should I have a problem with your friends?"

"When my best friend got married, her husband did not allow to meet with any of the friends because some of our friends are guys."

"I do not have any problem if you talk or meet with any of your friends. You are an independent person and have the freedom to do everything. You don't need my permission."

I was not interested in continuing the conversation. I asked, "Would you like to have something?"

"No thanks, I had coffee before leaving home."

I wanted to know what she thought about me. So I asked, "Are you happy with the engagement? Are you ready to get married?"

"I can do anything for my parents because they are very important to me."

"It is good that you respect your parents. But this is your life, and you are the one going to live your life. You should think about yourself first."

She ignored answering my question and said, "I am the center of my parents' world. I am happy to do whatever they ask me."

Her diplomatic answers annoyed me. She had the best parents in the world and was ready to sacrifice anything for them. Why should I come between the good parents and the good child? Why should I become a scapegoat?

I wanted an answer to I asked very straightforwardly. "What do you think about me? Do you like me?"

I was waiting for a diplomatic answer from her. As expected she said, "We will be able to understand each other only after we start living together." It was pointless to ask her anything else.

"Shall we leave now?" I asked.

It seemed as if she was a nursery class kid waiting for the school bell to ring.

"Do you want me to drop you home?"

"No, I can manage myself."

My mind was really disturbed. I was scared of the very same thing and that had happened. As people say that matches are made in heaven so there is no point in altering God's plans. If God has already planned everything for each one of us then why did he give us free will? Then why do people get divorced? Naziya was not exactly dumb but she was innocent and naïve. She was a clear mismatch for me. It would become impossible to spend life with her. Was there anyone who could understand me? I thought of talking about it to my maternal uncle but his reaction left me shocked.

"Look Ikku, nobody thinks so much when they are getting married. *Thawakkalthu Alalla*! (Put the faith in God's hands) If everyone thought as much as you do then nobody would ever get married. If you are not satisfied with your wife then you can have one more. Islam allows four marriages, you can keep more wives but if you leave the girl after engagement due to your stupid thoughts then the girl's future is at stake. She might not get a good proposal after that," he said.

I did not have any idea where it would end.

I tried to analyze God's reason behind sending the third angel in my life. Did God want to test my honesty and integrity? I remembered the words from a Guru on TV the other day. "This world is like a God's laboratory. Everyone is equal in his eyes and he wants to make the world a better place. He puts us in different situations and then expects us to take a wise decision.

Everyone in this world has some or the other problem. Some have health issues, some have monetary problems, some deal with relationship troubles and then some have problems with work.

When there is a phase of troubles in life, we think that only we are suffering and everyone else in the world is living happily. Each and everyone is constantly tested and God records our reactions.

There are seven levels in the heaven that God has created. Our actions decide that which level we will go after death. So whenever God tests us we should try our best to act right and make him happy.

I decided to return to Bangalore and when I told my mom about it she was not happy.

“You are supposed to be home for another week,” she said.

It was difficult for me to tell a lie. “My office is moved to another building and there are some things that we need to take care of before starting work there. I also need to get a medical checkup and document verification.”

Papa interrupted me and said, “If you are here for another week then we will finalize your wedding date. Then the venue can be booked for the ceremony. Also, I was thinking that it would be better if we get you married next month.”

I did not know why he was so eager to fix the wedding date so soon.

“Chicken price is low these days,” he said.

I angrily responded, "You can buy the chicken and keep it in the freezer for six months.”

I paused for some time and said, "I will come home for a couple of days in the coming week. Also, before finalizing the wedding date I need to take some important decision.”

“What do you mean?”

"I will explain in detail before fixing the date."

I boarded the bus and I was lost in my thoughts. I did not want to spoil Naziya’s life because of my decision.

I think the best thing to do when we are unable to reach a conclusion is to leave the confusion and think about it when our mind is at peace. I went to sleep.

Chapter 14

I reached Bangalore and was in a hunt for peace. I had not felt peaceful since past few years.

I was extremely happy during my college days. My only goal was to get a job and relationship was nowhere on my priority list. There was still tension about exams but my life was full of fun with my friends, movies, and soccer. I was however jealous when my friends began going out with girls. Now I feel pity for them.

When I finally found a job, I thought that I was secure and that it was the right time to find a girl.

The only advantage of work life is that I have enough money to take care of myself. I understood that money may bring happiness but it cannot give us peace. My college days will never return and it was a sad truth.

I went to a shopping mall as I needed some time off from worries. It was Phoenix mall on Whitefield Road. To my surprise, I saw someone known.

Yes, my first angel.

I envisaged that there was a possibility of meeting Rubina someday since we both lived in the same city.

She was alone and was window shopping. We were about to cross each other. She walked around confused and lost.

I was curious to know her reaction on seeing me.

I thought that she most probably would avoid me and walk away as if she had not seen me at all. Or maybe she would give me a smile and then head her own way. In the back of my mind, I felt that three years was a long time and she would have forgotten everything.

She looked at me and shouted, "Oh Iqbal...meeting you after a long time!"

She reacted as if she had seen a good old friend after a long time. It seemed that she had no bitterness for me anymore.

I said, "I am happy that at least you remember me."

She smiled and responded in a casual way. "How can I forget you? Nobody else haunted me as much as you did."

Then she asked, "How is life? Got married?"

I decided not to reveal about my life because I still did not make the final decision regarding that matter.

I said, "Life is going well. You did not accept my proposal, then how can I marry someone else? I decided to live the life as a bachelor." She smiled at my humor.

"What about you? Got married? I thought that I would see you with a baby."

"Even I decided not to get married after things did not work in between us," she chuckled.

I was a little surprised by the way she talked to me so openly. She always talked seriously to me, but there was a humorous touch in this conversation.

She did not show any attitude or arrogance. In fact, she had become very friendly and polite.

What happened to her? How did she change so much? Is it that people change in 2-3 years? Did she regret what she did to me? I had so many questions in me but tried to refrain myself.

"Iqbal I know that I was harsh towards you and was also arrogant sometimes. I can't go back in time and change whatever wrong I did but I sincerely wanted to apologize on meeting you. I am extremely sorry if you suffered in life because of me."

I could not believe that Rubina was asking for forgiveness.

I said, "I am so pleased to hear these words from you, but you do not need to be sorry. You did not do anything wrong."

"Please do not make me cry anymore."

She looked towards the watch and said, "I have an appointment in another half an hour. See you sometime."

She came back and asked, "Can you share your mobile number?"

I was completely clueless about God's plan for me. I never imagined in my wildest dreams that Rubina would ever come back into my life and then even apologize for her mistakes. I was still unsure that if she apologized genuinely or had any other hidden agenda behind it.

Were three years good enough to forget and forgive? I had no resentment towards Rubina but I always felt that she did not listen to me. I never wanted her to forcibly love me. I respected her decision and expected the same respect towards me. I did not regret losing the job because of her but I was hurt that I could not explain to her that how I felt. Even nations that are enemies listen to each other. I expected basic human courtesy.

No use of going back in time, I already moved on with my life.

If she had the guilt then why didn't she call me in all these years? We had so many mutual friends, thus getting the contact details was not a big deal.

I carefully observed her attitude. She took everyone for granted. Probably God tested her. I was not sure.

Her words of apologies spoke of the hurt that she must have gone through. When I tried to ask, she said, "Please do not make me cry anymore."

What did she mean? Had she cried a lot in life? The Rubina I knew would never cry. It was hard for me to believe. What was that she transformed her as a person?

I was curious to know about this.

I had her number saved. At one moment, I thought of calling her and then the other moment I decided to restrain myself.

Rubina was my first love and she was my first sweetheart. It was not easy to ignore her now especially when I had seen her softer side, Rubina 2.0.

I checked my phone and there was a message from Rubina.

"Hello Iqbal, it was nice to meet you."

That was the first message from Rubina. I responded, "Hello Rubina, it was a lazy day and I decided to go out. But my decision was obviously worth a treasure." I read the message after sending it. I wasn't sure why did I write that.

She replied, "Thank you so much. You have always been kind to me, but I did not have the wisdom to understand it. I am going through a rough patch in life and looking for a good friend to help me."

I had some emotional bond with Rubina, and if she was suffering then I could not give up on her. But my stupid mind kept reminding of the way she treated me in the past and how I became depressed after that.

I typed the message, "I am so sorry to hear that you are

going through personal issues. You can rely on me and I will do the best as I can."

She responded, "Thanks a lot. Are you free this evening? If possible, we can meet at a coffee shop."

We planned to meet but I did not have any excitement as compared to the first time I went out with her. As an exception, Rubina reached before me. She already reserved a table.

Rubina began the conversation, "I am happy after I met you today."

She was fatigued and looked like something haunted her.

She continued, "I made a decision against my parents and family to marry my best friend...my father strictly said that I have to move out of his home if I was going to marry against his wish."

She took a pause and then continued, "I was blindly in love with that guy and decided to leave my house."

"At that particular moment, I was so happy that I conquered my love. But, after knowing my partner's reaction, I felt a little weird. He said that we can register the wedding after six months. When I asked the reason he casually questioned me…what is the necessity to let the whole world know that we are getting married as it is the private decision between us."

She continued, "There was a dispute…he wants to have the live-in relationship and try out whether things are working out before getting married. But my ethics did not agree to do it, and there was a huge argument on that matter. I intimated him that I will not be able to go back to my home and asked him to find a way to resolve the conflict between us. Finally, we decided to stay together with a condition that we will not have any physical relationship until we get married. I was madly in love with that guy, and I thought that I will be able to convince him with time."

She took a deep breath and then spoke again. "But I failed. Things got worse, and we had a fight each and every day regarding this matter. I understood that he did not want to get married. One day I asked what kind of security I have. I am already away from my home as my parents are not going to accept me!"

Rubina stopped to drink water and then said, "When it was going to the worst stage, I decided to break up."

After I heard Rubina's story, I felt that none was to blame as it seemed like an ideological clash. I did not find anything wrong with the guy's approach. Perhaps he was born and brought up in a culture like that. He probably wanted to stay together to understand each other so that there isn't a bitter outcome at a later stage.

Even after staying together, he could not decide what he wanted. If I thought from Rubina's perspective, then she had no support as she had left her family for the guy and was now dependent on him. When they broke up, she was left alone. But fortunately, Rubina had a job.

Indian society is not mature enough to understand the new generation's expectations from marriage. In our country, the girls have to suffer if they try out such things like a live-in relationship.

I, however understood her reasons. I had no issue that she left her home and her parents to live with that guy. She followed her heart and tried her best to make the relationship work. When things got out of her control she quit the relationship. It was as simple as that.

Rubina said, "I hope you understand what I mean. We were just friends even if we were staying together. I may not be able to go back to the family now..."

After a pause, she continued, "Hope I do not sound like

an opportunist. Do you still have feelings for me?"

I was astonished by that sudden and unpredictable question and I looked at her eyes even though I understood her motive apparently. She clarified the question in much simpler words.

"I regret whatever I have done to you and had the guilt for not knowing you on a personal and real level. If you still have feelings for me, then I am ready to marry you."

I was a little perplexed and did not know how to answer the question. My first worry was that, I was already engaged to a girl that Rubina did not know about. I still hadn't made up my mind on that.

It was true that to some extent my heart still reached out to her after seeing her. After all, she was my first love. But if I was completely happy with my engagement then I wouldn't have been re-thinking.

I wanted to first decide my feeling about the engagement and only then I would be in a condition to answer Rubina's question.

I said, "Rubina, do you mind giving me some time to think about it?"

"Sure. Take your own time."

We left for the day after having coffee.

I was aware that Rubina came back into my life just because she did not have other options. Even though she apologized for her actions, she did not come back to me after understanding the depth of my love. If she was happy with her life, then she would not have even talked to me when I met her in the shopping complex.

I tried to relate our life with a simple theory in science. If the liquid boils at 100-degree centigrade then the same liquid freezes into ice if at 0 degrees.

My love towards Rubina was pure and pious. I did not feel such intensity even with Payal. The feeling with Payal resulted after understanding each other, but the feelings about Rubina was natural. The pain I felt after separating from Rubina was much more than what I felt after breaking up with Payal.

I was so lost in my thoughts that I did not realize when I slept. The alarm rang at 6:30 in the morning, I wanted to sleep some more but had to reach office on time. I was lazy to even get up so I skipped jogging and saved 15 minutes for a quick nap.

I was still sleepy at 6:45. Procrastination took over me and I skipped breakfast as well.

Early morning sleep is the best and I can sacrifice anything for it. I missed the alarm ring and finally woke up at 9:20. I jumped out of my bed and then rushed to the office quickly. I had no time to take bath and perfume came to my rescue. I was absent-minded. I reached near the bike and realized that I forgot to bring the keys. I had to go back home.

My grandmother never allowed to come back home once we leave as she believed it to be inauspicious. I used to laugh at her and make fun but the experience I had that day compelled me to believe in all her superstitions.

Something really tragic happened that day and my life was changed forever.

My mind still could not stop thinking about Rubina. I had a headache as I could not sleep properly and stopped the motorcycle near a tea stall. I was very late for office.

I then accelerated after some minutes and speeded up but I, unfortunately, had to stop at every signal and that irritated me even more. Bangalore roads are jam-packed in the mornings and are good enough to spoil anyone's morning.

Since it was peak time, the vehicles were not moving at all. I took a different route through the lanes.

It turned out to be the worst decision of my life.

It was a narrow lane with a lot of diversions and curves. People drove carelessly there and I took a right only to get hit by a truck.

I did not get any time to apply brakes. The truck was in speed and so was I. My bike smashed the bumper of the truck. Fortunately, I was wearing a helmet which saved my head but there was nothing to save my leg.

The truck tire ran over my right foot and crushed it completely. I could only see blood everywhere.

I was on road and waiting for help. Truck driver looked at me and ran away before the mob gathered.

My left arm was fractured and my jaw was broken. I needed someone to help me. I tried to stand up but could not.

Luckily an auto rickshaw stopped and people stepped out to help me. They tried to minimize the blood flow. Meanwhile, some people gathered and tried to push me inside the auto but my body did not fit and they called for an ambulance.

Someone splashed water on my face but I tried to remain conscious and gave my phone to people helping me. The ambulance did not reach in time so I was then carried to the hospital in a jeep. I fell unconscious on my way to the hospital. I had no idea for how long I was unconscious but when I opened my eyes, I was lying on the hospital bed and it took me some time to recollect the tragedy that had happened to me.

I was admitted to the ICU and was under observation. I did not have any idea about the seriousness of the injury. There was not much pain as I was on painkillers. The doctors checked me for my state of relief.

I could overhear their conversations, it was then I understood that I had minor fractures to my elbow but a critical injury to my right foot. I also came to know that I had undergone three major bone surgeries but they were all unsuccessful. I asked about my family members and then I finally got to meet them.

On seeing me, my mother cried out so loudly that the nurse had to warn her to not disturb other patients.

My father explained what the doctor had advised.

"Senior orthopedist Dr. Pai has done three critical operations. According to him, it is tough to rejoin the bone as it is completely damaged."

There was silence for some time, and then he continued,

"He advised to amputate the leg below the knee and fix an artificial one."

Dr. Pai came to me.

He heard us talk and then said, "You should not lose confidence, and in fact, you should be thanking God. It may be difficult to walk for a few days, but he will get used to it with time."

Then the doctor looked at me and asked, "Have you heard about Oscar Pistorius?"

I had no idea who he was talking about. "He is the man who lost both his legs and yet won Olympic medals in running. If you practice well then you too will be able to do all the activities that you did before like driving, swimming etc."

He spoke about a few more inspirational things and then finally said, "Only the approach and the attitude make the difference."

I was prepared for everything in life and did not lose faith in God. I never cried in front of my parents because I knew that they would not be able to bear the pain. We become strong when being strong is the only option left with us.

I firmly believe in destiny and whatever is bound to happen will happen. There was no point in blaming anyone so I tried to spread positivity around me.

I solaced people who tried to sympathize with my condition. "If something had happened to my backbone then I would not have been able to get up in this lifetime. We understand the value and preciousness of the life only if something major happens to us."

I pretended like it was not like a big deal even though it was breaking my heart.

I knew that the leg had to be amputated as there was no other way to save it. The doctors took me to the operation theatre and I was operated. I was under the effect of anesthesia and did not even realize that the surgery was over and my wounds were covered. I wanted to look at my leg but the doctors did not allow.

After keeping me under observation for 24 hours, the doctors shifted me from ICU to a private room. That was relaxing because I badly needed my family, friends and relatives around me.

Since it was 'hit and run' case, the police kept coming back for inquiries about the accident. I could not recall anything other than the complexion and the shape of the driver's body. We both were at mistake as we were driving without control. I did not blame the driver but would have forgiven him as well if he had helped me reach the hospital.

This world is extremely selfish but I was lucky to have found a few good people who helped me to get to the hospital. People hesitate to help the people involved in accidents because it involves medical and police formalities.

However, there are few people who take the pains even after knowing the consequences. My parents offered them money for bringing me to the hospital but they politely denied. I thanked them both from the bottom of my heart.

One of them was a guy called Chirag and the other one was Brajesh.

I was locked in a room of 10 by 8 for 30 days and I was dependent on others for everything. I was comfortable initially as I had my friends and relatives around me but after a few days my nights became long. One day when my parents had gone for some work, somebody knocked on the door of my room and then barged in. It was Payal and I did not know how to react because I had never thought that we would meet like this in a hospital.

"How are you?" I casually asked.

She responded in a low voice, "I am fine."

She began crying and could not control her emotions.

"How can God be so cruel to you?"

I let her cry because sometimes, we are peaceful only after venting out our emotions. I held her hand and said, "I feel so good when someone worries about me, and that is how I realize the importance of my life."

I looked into her eyes and then tried to calm her down. I said, "Do not worry. I am not going to suffer forever because of this tragedy. Doctors have suggested a few manufacturers of prosthetic legs. It will be trouble only in the initial days, and then it will be fine later."

There was a knock on the door and I thought it was my parents but to my surprise, I saw Rubina standing in front of me. I introduced them to each other. Payal recognized Rubina as I had already talked about her a lot.

Payal was shocked to see her as she had no idea about

what new had happened in my life.

Rubina asked all about the accident and I could see that she was remorseful. Payal looked at me confusingly and that's when I broke the ice between them. I had forgotten that Rubina had proposed to me and was waiting for the response. I realized that I should have informed her about the tragedy that happened to me. Payal and Rubina began talking about me.

Rubina explained that how did she come to know about my accident.

“I was waiting for your call after we met that day. I thought that you must be caught up with some work so I decided not to disturb you.”

I knew that she actually thought that I was not interested in marrying her and that is why she did not get back to me.

Rubina continued, "It was this one day I happened to meet Vivek, our friend from office. He told me all about an unfortunate incident.”

The door opened after some time and it was my fiancée Naziya. Naziya had been asking about my health all this while. It was a sheer coincidence and destiny's play that all my three angels were in the same room together. My parents had told that Naziya would come to visit me but I did not expect the other two women. I was puzzled. I did not know how to introduce Naziya to the girls as I had not told Rubina about my engagement. I had my own reasons but in a situation like that, I had to cover up. Naziya smiled and asked about my health and she looked at Payal and Rubina. I introduced them as my friends.

Rubina and Payal looked at me with puzzled eyes and I told them that Naziya was a relative.

I had to stop them from talking to each other as the truth at I was already engaged could be out in the open any moment.

I became nostalgic and started rewinding all the memories that I had created with these three Angels.

It felt like that I had found my soul mate when I met Rubina. I believed that God had sent an angel to take care of me and with whom I would live happily ever after.

The truth was that God had sent three Angels for me and there was a reason behind it. He had sent the first angel to make me a strong person and the second one to show me the beauty in the world.

I used to feel some kind of uneasiness when I used to wait for Payal but when I saw her smile, all my anger vanished. There was some unknown connection between our hearts. I could not fight with her for long and felt suffocated if I did not talk to her. There was some chemistry between us that always brought us back together always. A simple message with a smiley was sufficient to end the fight.

What was the purpose of the third angel? I started looking at life with a different perspective after meeting Naziya. Life is beautiful with only good people around her in Naziya's world. She doesn't judge people with intelligence before understanding them.

What is wisdom? According to me, 'wisdom' is a state when even the worst thing that could happen in life, does not affect to us. Every individual that comes across in our life, contributes to make us a better person. These three girls had contributed so much in my life and had helped me to reach to this stage. If I was able to take the personal tragedy of losing a leg positively, then it was all because of these three girls!

I also believed that there is a purpose to everyone's life, and I was discovering mine. So, did this personal tragedy change me as a person? Yes. It changed me a lot as a person and I started loving everyone, started caring for everyone, started thinking from other's perspective. I also became less demanding. Best part is, I started liking Naziya!

I was the one common thread amongst these three girls and I should have helped to strike the conversation. But, I was still in shock to see all the three of them together.

Payal said something sarcastically to Rubina, "I remember Iqbal saying that you are settled in the U.S."

I am was not sure how Rubina would respond. I did not want any kind of unpleasant moments in the hospital and said something in order to cover up.

I said, "Rubina had the opportunity to settle down in the U.S., but she did not opt for it because of her parents, I guess.."

I wanted them to leave soon and luckily, Rubina left saying that she had an urgent meeting in office.

Payal knew that there was something fishy. She asked, "Your name is Naziya, right? You are Iqbal's fiancée?"

Then, she looked at me and then asked, "Why didn't you introduce her as your fiancée?"

I managed the situation by saying something. "I was not sure whether Naziya would like to be introduced as my fiancé."

Payal turned towards me and asked, "What do you liked the most in Naziya?"

I cleared my throat and said, "Obviously, Naziya's innocence attracted me. She is so humble and a very good human being. She cares for me like a child and her concern sounds very genuine. That is how I started liking her."

We three talked for some time and they both had to leave after the visitors' time was over. Life is so unpredictable!

Chapter 15

I returned to my hometown after spending 45 days in the hospital. My solitude continued as I was on strict bed rest for three months. It was not the physical pain but the mental agony had taken over me. I started comparing my life with that of others, normal people who could move around freely without any support. I even began to regret all the things that I could not do and would never be able to do again in life. Mustafa and Sajid came to visit me. I shared my feelings with Mustafa. He knew that I always loved playing football and was crazy after it.

"You can start playing games like Table-Tennis and Badminton where the foot movement is minimal. Then you can gradually switch to other games according to your health condition."

That sounded good to me.

I sent an email to the project manager and informed in detail about the accident. He assured me all the co-operation. In all these days, Naziya called me several times in a day. I started liking her, she had genuinely cared me.

The plasters were removed after the wound healed completely and my prosthetic leg was fixed in place. I was instructed to first walk slowly and then try to do other activities. I dressed up and then wore the shoes that supported my artificial leg.

The leg seemed real and anyone who did not know that I had met with such an accident would not come to know about it. However, I needed to practice walking like a baby. I tried to take tiny steps with the help of crutches. I tried my best but the pain was immense and after failed attempts I gave up. The man from the prosthetic clinic asked me try some more.

He said, "It will be difficult to walk if you do not practice well."

I gathered all my strength and then walked a couple of steps, but fell to the floor badly. Everyone in the family rushed to help me stand and then settled me on a sofa. I asked them to remove the leg as I could not bear the pain. They removed it and found blood clots. I decided to practice slowly until I got used to it.

Papa lost his temper and talked to the nursing staff in an extremely harsh manner.

In the Meantime Rubina called up and asked about my health, she even requested to meet when I would be in Bangalore.

Life became hell as I was dependent for everything. Most of the time, Asif and Fouziya were not at home as it was the end of their academic year. They were both busy preparing for exams. Loneliness began haunting me and I felt like a fish without water. Being isolated from work, friends and passion had an adverse effect on my self-confidence and I began doubting my capabilities. I was really scarred internally.

When we have self-confidence, we are driven to achieve the impossible but when the opposite happens, everything starts to seem gloomy. I looked at the fan and thought that it would fall over me and whenever I used electric appliances I thought I would definitely get electrocuted.

Our mind is a deep mystery and it is tough to change our outlook easily. When our thoughts start putting us in a comfort zone then it is not easy to achieve anything at all. My first step towards regaining confidence was to become self-sufficient and I worked hard to walk without anyone's help. I tried to reason the tragedy. Maybe it was because I might have done something evil to someone. In all those days, my faith in God strengthened and I felt that it was all to purify my soul and make me a better person.

I had set goals for myself that were achievable, like joining back office and gradually getting back to my normal life. I succeeded at taking a tiny step and my parents' happiness knew no bounds. They encouraged me like a baby who was being taught to walk again.

I was focusing on my recovery and had no worries about the wedding but Papa was anxious. He kept coming to me with options for wedding cards.

He showed me a card and read it out loud, "Everyone in the family is cordially invited." Then he stopped to stare at me and asked, "Is this necessary?"

I ignored him completely.

Mom said, "We need to request the girl's family to postpone the marriage date for another six months. They are aware of the condition and hopefully, will agree."

Papa responded, "Yes, we already booked the wedding hall. If we are informing them well in advance, they can book it for another date."

They both asked my opinion and I said, "My immediate priority is to become fit. Wedding is not even on my list."

Mom said, "Nothing happened to you. You are absolutely okay."

My parents came to a decision of calling Naziya's parents to fix another date for the wedding.

Papa got a call from Naziya's father. He said that he wanted to visit us.

Papa responded, "Let us meet this Sunday?"

They both agreed to meet on the weekend, but Naziya's father politely refused to have food at our place.

I smelled a rat and said, "I have a feeling that they are coming to give some unpleasant news.

"Why do you think like that? Is it because they refused to have dinner at our place? Maybe they don't want to trouble us," mom said.

I said, "Let us wait and see."

Naziya's father and uncle arrived. Their faces looked pale and I could see no excitement like I had seen on the engagement day.

They came to the topic straightaway and said, "It can be appalling for you and we are sorry if it hurts but some of our family members have serious objections to the marriage as Iqbal's condition and life has completely changed. We tried to convince them a lot but failed to reason. Finally, we all reached the decision of calling off the wedding."

My Dad could not digest it easily.

He said, "Nothing has happened to Iqbal. He is mentally, physically and financially stable. He will be able to go to the office and do all other work that he did before. He needs mental support at the moment and this can worsen his condition."

Naziya's Uncle answered, "We truly understand your feelings, and we regret from the bottom of the heart but we had only this option."

My mom was listening to everything from the dining

area. In our family, the females are not allowed to be a part of important discussions. She rushed into the living room and began shouting.

“Is there even any value of promises? What if all this happened after the marriage, then would you have broken the marriage? Allah knows everything and he is watching.”

Her emotional outburst was understandable and I tried to calm her and asked her to go to another room. The next formality was to return the ornaments and dresses. My father was a little hesitant to take everything back. I went ahead and took it from them.

I said, "Please excuse us. My parents think that I am upset. I am not. I totally understand being in your shoes. You need not be sorry for whatever has happened."

Our guests did not say a word and left without even taking a sip of the juice that we had served on the table. I could see awkwardness in their eyes.

What is my worry? Even if my parents shout out to the world that I was normal, the society would not accept me. I knew that the society would always treat me as a physically disabled person. The reality was that the girl who commits to marry finally denied so there was no chance that any other girl was going to accept me. My parents loved me so they did not say the obvious but I accepted the hard truth.

Naziya's uncle and father were looking for a chance to leave. My dad had still not recovered from the stroke and kept looking at the floor without uttering a single word.

“What is the girl's opinion? She is the one who has to live with him. If she has no problem then it won't be wise to call off the wedding.” My father asked straightforwardly.

The question did not go down well with Naziya's father and he bluntly said, “Naziya has no different opinion. She will oblige to the decision of elders in the family.”

“We have to leave now as we got some other appointment."

Before leaving, they shook hands with me and said, “May Allah bless you."

When we are so upset, what we usually do? We start blaming each and everything in the world and that is exactly what my mom was doing. It was so hard to convince her.

After Naziya's father and uncle had left, I received a call from her. I did not want my mom to hear the conversation, so I went outside.

“My father must have visited you...” She was stammering and I could sense hesitation in her voice.

"Yes, your papa and uncle had come to our place, they left some time back."

She continued speaking in broken sentences. "I do not know what to say. I am so sorry for everything that has happened."

She took a pause and then continued. "It was not my decision to call off the wedding and my opinion holds no value in my family."

"Naziya, if you are sorry because I am upset, then please don't do that...I am not disappointed at all. I do not blame your parents or relatives for breaking the engagement. Your life is important to them. But when you are saying that you are not allowed to put forward your opinion, I feel a little awkward. I do not know if the problem is on your side or your parent's side. Try to make an attempt to put across your view because it is your life and your decision is also important."

I knew that it was tough to explain it to her and then hung up after trying my best not to hurt her. “You can consider me as your good friend and I will always be there for you. All the best. Goodbye."

I decided to leave home and thought that the new workplace would boost my mood. My mom worried about my fitness and health.

“My stay at home is not going to help me.” I persuaded mom.

I actually wanted to talk to Rubina. I knew that things had changed completely since the day she proposed to me. Naziya who was engaged to me broke the relationship due to my life-changing tragedy, so there was no chance that Rubina was going to accept me. Rubina called me up a couple of times when I was on bed rest. She was concerned about my health and wanted to discuss something really important when I would return to Bangalore. What did she want to talk about? Maybe she realized that the reason for the accident was improper sleep and she was the reason for keeping me awake till late. Was she feeling guilty? I booked bus tickets and packed my bags. My parents were a little hesitant to leave me alone. They knew that I was still not completely fine but papa allowed and dropped me to the bus stand.

After reaching Bangalore, I called Rubina and she suggested a place to meet. I was clueless about the agenda of this meeting but still headed towards the restaurant. Rubina looked pleasant but there was some kind of uneasiness on her face. She, however, looked way better than the last time I saw her in the hospital. She was very exhausted and worn out then.

I said, "You look happy now."

"I was roaming around like a zombie when we met the last time. But, my parents understood my situation, and they have accepted me. After all, parents are parents. They forgive all our mistakes and love us unconditionally."

"I am truly happy for you."

She said, "I am sorry…last time...I came with a marriage proposal..."

I had no idea what she wanted to say, there was silence for a minute and then she said, "I have already told about my father and how he is so strict and stubborn. He knows that I chose a wrong guy earlier and will never allow me to marry someone of my choice. He is looking for marriage proposals for me."

She avoided eye contact with me. I looked at her hands, she was shivering.

She then looked me into the eyes and said, "I am sorry Iqbal, I cannot hurt my father again. I know that you will get a really nice girl. Please forget everything. I will always be a very good friend to you."

"I respect your decision. I am not sure if the reason you gave me is the one that has compelled to change your decision but I am happy that at least this time you were courteous enough to inform me. It is terrible when someone we love, starts ignoring us. We are then tempted to take extreme actions out of frustration. Thanks for considering me your friend. I will always be there to help you."

I took a long breath and then cracked a joke. "You must be thinking that what kind of a help can a physically damaged person be? Actually, I have an excellent network of people who can get things done."

I decided to lighten up the environment and asked about her work.

"It is very important to respect our parents and they are the only ones who accept us even when we take them for granted."

Rubina still seemed gloomy. I tried to cheer her up and said, "You are a pretty girl who has a nice job. You will get anyone whom you like but whenever you choose someone, do not only look for appearance or financial stability. It is very important to find someone who loves you unconditionally. I appreciate your decision of leaving the marriage-related matters into your parents' hands. I am sure that they will find someone suitable for you."

It was THE END of my story with Rubina. I recalled all the time that I spent with her and laughed remembering a few incidents. I still doubted that her father was the reason behind changing her mind. If Rubina wanted to marry me then she could have at least tried.

I knew Rubina very well. She was a persistent and determined girl. She did not say a word regarding any chance that we could try. I knew that the real reason was obviously my health condition. She cleverly put the blame on her father because she was not ready to take the burden. But if I think from her perspective then she had not one any wrong because we were not emotionally attached.

I knew that Rubina was not a bad girl but she definitely is a self-centered girl. When I proposed her for the first time, she was not interested in me and behaved according to that. When she came back to me for the second time when she was badly looking for a support and proposed me. When some tragedy happened to me, she thought she could get better options and thus left. Rubina must be dreaming for the ideal partner but our life is meaningful when we are doing something for others or living for someone. I did not show any remorse and calmly let her go. Then, I headed towards the home.

I went to bed but could not get any sleep. How did my life change so drastically? A few months back, I had options and I had to choose the best one for me and all of a sudden I became an untouchable and nobody was ready to be with me. We think that everything will remain the same and we'd be happy but a small incident is good enough to take everything away from us.

My respect towards women did not reduce even an inch, after I had some bad experiences. I firmly believe that all the women should be treated as Angels.

A man is usually judged by how he treats his wife and mother. Similarly a country is judged by how the men in the country treat their women. Every father wants to treat his daughter with special care. If you want your daughter to be treated as an Angel by everyone, then you should treat other women with the level of respect and dignity that befits an Angel.

How many times it happens in our life where we give up completely and as time passes some strange power appears and makes everything perfect?

Some call it a Miracle. It happened many times in my life. I had almost given up on life after the disappointing job hunt, and after the bad experience with Rubina. There was some angel or some strange power which helped me to overcome these events. This power is beyond the control of human technology or knowledge.

When something happens beyond the contol of technology or medical science, we call it as Miracle. This is the reason I am truly spritual and a firm believer of destiny.

The next day, I saw a message from Payal. She had written that she wanted to meet me immediately.

I quickly headed to our old meeting spot and I was anxious to see her because my faith in God was shaking. I wanted to meet someone close to my heart.

Whenever I used to go to Payal with a problem, I would come back as a different person. I felt that she had hands that could bless. She was the true angel that God had sent with a healing touch. When I was low and depressed in life, she was the one who inspired me to live and not give up on loving people.

I know that it is selfish to hope anything as we had broken up for good and also that she was going to marry someone else. When Payal saw me, she rushed towards me and hugged me tightly.

Payal started crying badly and I allowed her to do that because I felt safe in the bond I shared with her.

I looked at her in confusion and she said, "Iqbal, I cannot marry anyone else other than you."

"I called my fiancé and told him that I would not be able to do justice to our relationship and he appreciated my decision."

She stopped to take a breath and then said, "I came to know that your engagement was called off. Trust me. My decision is not driven by sympathy. I have decided to marry you from all my heart."

"Do you have any idea about what you are doing? You are throwing away a better life and tying yourself to a liability. You will be playing with your family's happiness as they are planning your wedding."

"I realized that I will be happy only with you, and you cannot be a liability to me at any stage of my life. She came closer to me and then said, "I cannot think of a life without you."

I understood that her emotional outburst was deep-rooted and I experienced what true love feels like, which knows no boundaries, religion, status or language. Those were the wonderful words that everyone wants to hear. At that moment, I did not expect anything else from this life. Payal is a true gem and 'My True Angel' in life. This was the moment where I found meaning to my life. I wish that everyone in this world should have a person like Payal in their lives.

She looked at me and then said, "There is a problem."

I looked at her confusingly.

"Your parents did not want us to marry. We both know what they did last time. How will we convince them now?"

I answered her without even thinking for a second. "My parents realized that I am not going to get a good proposal and I am sure they are not going to make an issue this time."

She hugged me and I felt the warmth of her love pierce through my chest. In that moment, I thought that whatever happens in life happens for good, including my accident. The worst times in my life helped me understand the intentions of people in a better way. We all work hard to make a name, an identity for us. We compromise our quality time so that we can achieve some success but I understood that everything is temporary. We are so busy in our own lives that we fail to understand the pain felt by our loved ones. We are unable to differentiate between a fake and a real friend because we hardly take out time to develop a genuine relationship.

When we were young, our goals revolved around getting a dream job, making a lot of money and leading a comfortable life. How many of us had the goal of having good relationships with other people? Not even a single one of us thought of creating a helpful network for us. We are so stuck in the wars of religion, caste, language, and color that it gets difficult to take a moment to look for good people around us. We spend our days and nights in order to create a bank balance and build a house. But, we do not realize that our true assets are true relationships.

This was my love story, and just like other Indian parents, my parents created huge hurdles in it. However, they realized that it was for the best. Just how they say in the end of a fairy tale- Payal and Iqbal lived happily ever after.

Thank God, for blessing the love of my life. One of the

happiest things on earth is marrying someone who loves you more.

I never hated anyone in life, each and every person that crossed my path has only helped me to become a better person, especially Rubina and Naziya, I do not call them selfish or opportunists because they took a wise decision for their future. I would have never understood the value of other people in life without them. I call both of them, my angels. I do not have words for my sweetheart, Payal, as no word can ever entirely hold the weight of my love for her.

My complicated and puzzled love life found a glorious destination. After joining the new company, I now have a steady career. I walk like any other person with a real leg. I can now run, swim, drive and do all other activities. One day Payal asked, "We have decided to follow our own religion we were born into but what about our children?"

I said, "Let them decide when they grow up. I believe religion is something that should not be forced upon anyone. When a person has the freedom to choose the career, then why can't s/he choose the religion? Relationship with God should be a private matter. The motto of every religion was to guide people to the righteous path. It is losing its core value because of people's ego"

Zubaida Aunty did not consider it a wedding. She called it an illicit relationship that is not valid according to Islamic customs.

"How can you say that you both are married when the *Nikah* was not performed? Also, the girl is still Hindu. There will be harsher punishment in *Qabr* (graveyard) for the illicit relationship," said Zubaida Aunty.

I wanted to ask her that how many times she had been to the graveyard but I decided to turn a deaf ear. Ignoring is the best way to deal with such people.

Many of my friends did not believe me when I told them that I convinced my parents.

"This is the 8th wonder. How did it happen?" Senthil asked.

I said, "Haven't you ever read or heard that parents even donate essential organs to their children if needed? Ultimately, their child's happiness is everything for each parent. Initially, it is difficult for families with orthodox thinking to accept that there is something above society."

One day I asked Payal, "Why did you cry when I first kissed you?"

"You will never understand that, as you are a guy."

I haven't figured out the reason till this date.

Every love story is beautiful but our love story is special because it has a message to convey. The message is so important for today's generation. More and more inter-caste and inter religion marriages could be one solution to our problems.

We Indians mix religion with everything. When someone says that his name is Abdullah or Narayan, we are quick to assume their religion and create an image of that person in our mind according to our sensibilities towards that religion. We do not even try to know them on a personal level before judging them. Every other Facebook argument is about religion.

Let us love people unconditionally, irrespective of their religion, color or language. Good and bad people exist in all religions and if somebody does any wrong then the entire community should not be targeted and blamed.

If I am successful in bringing about a positive change in the perspective of even one of the readers of this story then my mission would be successful.

About the Author

Irshad Talakala, presently working as IT specialist in IBM Bangalore. He worked with Tech Mahindra, Tata Technologies and Aeronautical Defence Agency earlier. He has a passion to write and is a frequent writer of blogs. This is his first attempt to write a full length novel. He is basically from a place called Talakala which is in northern part of Kerala. He finished his primary education from Kasaragod, Kerala and higher education from Mangalore, Karnataka. Other than writing, he likes to explore different varieties of food.

You can get in touch through irshad.thalakala@gmail.com